THE TF

THE TEMPLERS

By

R. Howard Trembly

Cover Illustration By

Morris Grover

of

CoverUp

Other Books by R. Howard Trembly

Madigan

A Transgression in Time

Killer I Am

And more books coming soon.

This book is dedicated to all the heroes that fought in the American Civil War. Whether Confederate or Union, these men, boys, and sometimes women believed so strongly in what they were fighting for that they gave up their lives in defense of these beliefs, often leaving families back home that became embroiled in their own battle to survive. But no matter whose side they were on, they all had one thing in common.

They were Americans!

THE TEMPLERS

By

R. Howard Trembly

Chapter I

The gray digger stood on its hind legs and scanned the field before him, making little clicking noises to let the others in his community know he was still on guard while they grazed the few remaining blades of grass from around their dens. Turning his body first one way, then another, the ground squirrel tried to make up his mind whether to give the warning call or take the chance to stand and watch. For the moment he chose to wait.

Off in the distance two small specks had appeared, slowly moving closer. Still the squirrel waited and watched, curious about the distant dots coming nearer with each minute. First he would stand on his hind legs, then drop to all fours, his busy tail standing out behind him like a flag. He repeated the maneuver time after time as if somehow his powers of observation would increase each time he stood up.

The specks were now taking on shape and the big gray became more alert, no longer going down to all fours, but standing rigid and erect while contemplating the two humans with renewed interest. These creatures were different from most he had seen--one was small, much smaller than the other. His full attention was on them as they walked in a line directly toward where the gray digger stood. The smaller humanoid followed the larger one, bumping into him when he stopped short. And so these two humans came, closer and closer until they were but a hundred yards away from the little gray sentinel on the mound.

As the animal watched with fascination, the two humans lowered themselves to the ground so that one was on his elbows and knees while the other sat upright. There was something else different about these two humans the squirrel didn't notice earlier, the one in front carried a long slender stick the squirrel had come to know as the stick that brought death to his community, but known by humans as a rifle. Not any rifle, but a .32 caliber squirrel rifle with double set triggers, able to shoot the head off a squirrel at fifty yards or more. Of course, this was not information the gray digger knew. It only knew that when the stick barked, death followed for one of its own.

The morning had dawned cool and damp, the remnant of last night's rain showing as small puddles on the ground. As the sun crept up from behind the low green hills in the distance, the ground was drying fast, giving off little puffs of steam that rose a few feet into the air, then vanished as if some unseen magician's wand was zapping them into nothingness. The air had that crisp sweet smell that comes with the first days of spring, giving off notions of what was to come later in the summer. Here and there yellow daffodils stood straight and tall, their bright smiling faces turned to catch the first rays of the morning sun. To Josh Templer it seemed the perfect morning for hunting, or just plain living for that matter.

He had been walking along with his rifle slung under his arm when all of a sudden he saw the biggest gray digger he'd ever laid eyes on. It stood not more than a couple of hundred yards distance scrutinizing them as they walked along. Josh froze in his tracks, not bothering to tell Henry to do the same. It was Henry's misfortune to walk right into the butt of Josh's rifle. Josh, being so much taller than his little brother, was carrying the rifle right at eye level to Henry. The rifle butt took Henry across the left cheek in a glancing blow that caused him at once to move forward and to the right while at the same time letting out an "ouch!"

Josh, hearing the complaint from his brother, quickly turned to see what happened. As he did, the barrel of his rifle caught Henry a good whack across his forehead, almost knocking him off his feet.

"What'd you do that for?!" Henry yelled, rubbing his head with his hands.

"I didn't do it on purpose. Pay attention after this. Now get down real slow. There's a big one over yonder and he'll make a meal all by himself." Surprisingly the digger hadn't moved.

The two boys hunched down. "I'll wait here for you," Henry said, as Josh lowered himself to his hands and knees, cradling the rifle in the crook of his arms while he crawled closer to his intended prey. The big gray just stood there and watched as Josh, the hunter, crawled ever so slowly forward, stopping whenever the squirrel showed signs of becoming nervous. Closer and closer he crawled, not daring to take his eyes off the little animal that now appeared more like a stone statue than a living, breathing mammal.

There is a thing known to hunters as buck fever, and it now had Josh firmly in its grasp. The closer he got to the squirrel, the narrower his vision became. His heart, beating much faster than normal, felt like it was going to burst from his chest. If the sound of it's beat didn't give him away first and frighten the digger, he might get a shot at this solitary denizen of the grassy meadows.

Josh was no longer a mere boy going after a lone squirrel, but a hunter stalking his prey. Nothing else mattered. There were no smells, no noise, save that of his heart beating faster and faster. Nothing else but the squirrel, unmoving upon its mound of dirt, from which at any moment Josh knew it could disappear at the slightest provocation.

Onward Josh crawled, hearing nothing, seeing only the prey, feeling nothing but the excitement of the hunt, the adrenaline flowing strong in his veins. Finally, after what seemed like hours, he was ready to make the kill. Slowly, ever so slowly, he moved his rifle into the shooting position. The front sight curved around in the air to bear on the squirrel while the butt of the rifle came to Josh's shoulder in one smooth motion, aligning the rear sight with its partner at the end of the long barrel.

He carefully brought the hammer back in one smooth, steady motion, while the click of the hammer being cocked sounded like a cannon going off in his ears. Funny how the sound came rushing in where there was nothing before. The squirrel jerked at the noise, then froze into the statue it was before, only its nose twitching to show that it was even alive. Josh started putting pressure on the rear trigger that allowed the front one to become a hair trigger. Just as he began squeezing the Set Trigger, the gray digger abruptly dropped out of sight down its burrow to safety.

Josh couldn't believe his eyes. "Did you see that little rascal?" he said to no one in particular. "He waited till I had him in my sights, then he's gone just as I'm going to lay him low." Coming to his feet Josh looked around for Henry. There he was, right where he'd left him twiddling with a piece of grass, not having noticed anything of the last few minutes.

"Henry, didn't you even see what happened?"

Henry looked up at his big brother, but instead of saying anything, a big grin broke out on his face.

"What's so funny?"

"Nothin'." Henry's smile erupted into a laugh.

Josh stood there trying to figure out what was going on when the faintest whiff of a pungent odor reached his nostrils. He sniffed the air trying to determine what it was, wrinkling his nose at the offending smell. Then it hit him. Ever so slowly, he looked down at the front of his clothes; not wanting to see what he knew would be there.

"Darn!" he cursed. "I crawled right through a cow pie and that big gray squirrel watched me do it. Darn!" As Josh bent down to get a handful of grass to wipe himself clean, he glanced toward the mound on which the gray squirrel had been standing. There, only its head visible above the dirt, was the big gray watching Josh's every move. Then just as quickly as before, it vanished deep into its burrow.

"I got cow manure all over myself and I bet that digger was just waiting for me to do it! He's probably down in his hole laughing still! Come on, Henry. I'm through hunting for today, but I'll get that digger if it takes me forever." Josh pulled the little rifle up to his shoulder and quickly fired a shot into the mound of dirt where he last saw the squirrel's head. "That's just a warning of what's to come!" he yelled, before turning to his brother. "Now you better not tell anyone about this, you hear?"

Henry looked over to the mound where the gray digger now stood watching the two humans again. He laughed at the sight. Josh was not amused.

"What do I tell Ma when we don't bring no squirrels home? And besides, she's sure to smell you before you get within ten feet of the house."

"Aw, I don't smell near that bad."

"You do too!" Henry giggled.

"Well, I won't. I'll rinse my clothes in the water trough, then keep out of sight till they dry."

"What about no squirrels?"

"Tell her you got bored and decided to come home. I'll think of what to tell her later."

"You gonna lie to Ma?"

"Not lie, just bend the truth a little like Uncle Jack used to do."

"Them was stories Uncle Jack was tellin', that he just made up. Everybody knows that. And why shouldn't I tell her? I ain't got manure all over me."

Josh looked at his little brother for a long minute. It wasn't hard to see he was over a barrel and Henry knew it. It wasn't so much that his mom would mind, it was the embarrassment of the whole thing. And he could just hear his pa laugh and joke about it for a week of Sundays. Good thing Pa went to town for supplies this morning, so all he'd have to do is keep out of sight of Ma until his clothes dried and that would be the end of it. He could always say a coyote or something chased all the diggers away and he'd waited for them to come back out, but they never did. Of course, Henry was still another matter.

"Because I'll give you my pocket knife," Josh finally said.

"Cough it over," Henry demanded, holding out his hand in anticipation.

"Now, you better keep quiet!"

As the two boys walked home they saw in the distance someone leaving their house. It appeared to be a girl but they couldn't quite tell.

"Wonder who that is?"

"I can't tell, but I can go find out if you want me to," Henry offered.

"Just stay here, we'll find out later." Josh knew what his little brother had in mind and didn't like it, not one bit.

"I'm going to be in the barn, so you just keep your mouth shut!"

"If Ma asks, I won't lie," Henry said defiantly, knowing full well he had his big brother in a hard place.

"All right, what else you want?"

"Do my chores for a week?"

Josh gritted his teeth, holding back the anger he was starting to feel at the blackmail he was being subjected to. "Okay," Josh said reluctantly through clenched teeth, "but keep your mouth shut!" He raised his clenched fist to make the point very clear to his little brother.

When they got close to the house Josh ducked behind the barn until Henry went inside. Waiting five minutes to make sure all was clear, he took off his soiled clothes. After dunking them in the water trough and swishing them around to wash all the manure off, he found a place to hang them inside the barn where they couldn't be seen from outside but still allowed the sun to shine on them through a window high in the wall. Josh was glad it was still early in the spring and he still wore his long johns. At least he wasn't totally naked. Now all he had to do was find a place in the hayloft to lie down and wait for his clothes to dry. He was just settling in for a nap when he heard something move behind him.

"Well, I can see you're glad to see me, aren't you Josh?" Josh jumped to his feet and turned to face Mary Jane Horstead.

"What are you doing here, Mary Jane?" Josh yelled, as he grabbed a burlap sack off a nail on the wall and wrapped it around him, at the same time glancing a peek outside to see if his shout of surprise was heard.

Mary Jane was tall for a girl in these days when most women were short and stout. Stout definitely was not what you'd call her. She was slim, with a small waist and large but well-shaped bosom, which she made a point to show off by removing the top three buttons of whatever blouse she was wearing. Her hips weren't large either, but well-proportioned for her build, swinging in just the right way to attract attention from all the men that still had a heart beating in their chest.

The women hated her, while the men loved it when she came walking down the road in their direction, her long blond hair bouncing around her shoulders. And her hair wasn't all that was bouncing when she walked, causing the hearts of old and young men alike to beat even faster.

"I'm looking for one of our pigs. He ran away this morning and I thought he might have come this way, so I thought I'd look around your place to see if he came in here."

"In our barn? In the hayloft? We wouldn't have your pig in our barn! You know that, Mary Jane!" he said, trying to sound indignant at her suggestion, but not quite carrying it off. After all, he was standing in front of her wearing nothing but a pair of long johns and a burlap sack.

"I know," she smiled, "but I really didn't come into the barn to find pigs. I came in here to see you, Josh. And by the way you're dressed, I'd say I picked the right time, too."

"How'd you know I was in here?"

"Henry."

"That figures. Just wait till I get my hands on that little traitor!"

The longer Mary Jane and Josh faced each other, the more flustered he became. Josh realized that he was perspiring, and it wasn't that warm in the barn.

"What are you up to, Mary Jane?" Josh demanded. He was getting worried now. Mary Jane didn't have the best reputation, and Josh didn't want to be seen with her, or any other member of her family for that matter.

The Horsteads were pig farmers, and it was often said that their pigs were cleaner than the Horstead family itself. If you ever got downwind of them, you knew why they were given a wide berth. They weren't just dirty--they stunk. They also had the habit of letting other people's things stick to their fingers, and nobody liked a thief.

Mary Jane was the exception to the family. She was clean and well kept, and although she didn't smell pretty, like the dance hall women Josh had heard about, she didn't smell bad either. You could say she didn't smell at all.

It was rumored, however, that she liked to seduce boys that were younger than her. It was only a rumor, as nobody ever admitted to being one of her victims. Standing here before him, she did seem kind of appealing to Josh, who was two years her junior. Josh hadn't had much to do with girls, and what he was feeling now was unfamiliar to him.

Mary Jane slowly moved closer to him. Josh froze, not knowing what to do. He couldn't very well run out of the barn dressed the way he was, and when Josh thought about it, he didn't really want to anyway. For a moment they faced each other, neither of them saying anything. Mary Jane took another step closer to Josh.

"Want to do something, Josh?"

"What?" asked Josh, suspecting full well what she meant.

"Oh, something that makes you feel good inside." Josh blushed. Mary Jane took another step closer. "I'll show you. You won't have to do anything."

Josh became aware of a strange feeling slowly creeping over him. Mary Jane was now less than a foot away from him. She deliberately reached over and pulled the sack from around his waist. Josh wanted to run, but at the same time stay. Mary Jane smiled at him as she purposely slid her hand into the front of Josh's long johns.

Josh became flushed, hot and cold at the same time. What was happening to him? Mary Jane pulled him to the back of the barn where hay was piled in large, soft piles.

"Come with me, Josh, I'll teach you."

It was like a dream as together they sank into the hay.

His clothes were still damp when Josh dressed in them. Mary Jane had left through the back door of the barn. Josh waited until she was completely gone from sight, then walked into the house. Ma was busy at the cook stove, stirring something in a big black kettle. It smelled good and Josh was surprised at how hungry he was.

"Did you see Mary Jane out there anywhere, Josh?" Ma kept right on stirring while she waited for Josh to answer.

Josh's heart abruptly skipped a beat and his mouth felt dry like sandpaper. Did his ma know about him and Mary Jane? How could she? Did Henry spy on them in the barn and then tell his ma? He doubted it as his ma was much too calm to have known something like that. But why was she asking about Mary Jane? He'd just have to wait and see. Until then, he'd just play dumb.

"What's she doing around here, Ma?"

"Her folks came by earlier lookin' for her, said she left this morning to find one of their pigs. Didn't really know where to look, just going from place to place. Could just be using that as an excuse to see what things they can lay their hands on. I'm sorry to say they're not the most trustworthy folks, and I fear their daughter's not much better. You better stay clear of that Mary Jane if you see her. She's real trouble."

Josh looked at the back of his ma's head. Did she suspect what had happened? Josh was hoping she wouldn't turn around. If she did, she would see the whole story written on his face. She kept on with her cooking.

"Yeah, I saw her walking over by the woods heading in the direction of her place."

"You stay away from her, son," Ruth Templer admonished, "she can ruin a sweet boy like you."

"What do you mean, Ma?" Josh asked before he thought better.

"Nothing, son. Wait till you're a might older."

A thought crossed Josh's mind--*too late for that.*

"By the way, Henry told me all about what happened while you two were out hunting."

"I asked him not to say anything." Josh was starting to get mad inside.

"Well, it's a good thing he did or we'd have no supper tonight when your pa gets home. Henry said you'd stay out all day waiting for the squirrels to return after the coyote scared them all away. But I knew they'd stay under ground for a long spell, so I made other plans. Maybe next week you can try again."

So, his little brother wasn't so bad after all, at least if you paid him, Josh smiled to himself. Not a bad little brother at all.

"Ma, if you don't need me for anything, I'm kind of tired and would like to take a nap.

"Go ahead, son, you sound tired."

"By the way, where is Henry?"

"Henry walked down the road to meet Pa on his way back from town. Knowing Henry, he's thinkin' he'll get some of the sweets Pa's bound to bring back. You know Henry and his sweet tooth."

The snorting of the horses woke Josh from his nap. He had been dreaming of a wonderful fair-haired maiden fondling him all over. Now awake he was a little bothered by the dream.

"Pa's home!" Ma called. "You better go help him with the supplies."

Josh would rather have gone back to sleep, but instead he went out to the wagon to help with the unloading. Pa had gone to town early that morning, as he did once or twice a month. This time he had news for the family.

"Gonna be a barn dance next week at Joe and Millie's place to celebrate their new grandson. I hear people will be comin' from miles around. They're going to roast a whole steer, so they said come with a empty stomach and a good appetite. And there'll be plenty of pretty girls there, too. With most of the older boys gone off to war, there's bound to be more girls than boys." John Templer looked over at his son and smiled, "Maybe you'll get your first kiss, Josh."

Or a whole lot more. Mary Jane's sure to be there, Josh thought as he smiled inwardly. Outwardly, he just shrugged it off and went ahead unloading the supplies from the back of the wagon.

Chapter II

You could hear the fiddlers a mile away, as wagon after wagon brought families and friends together. Josh tried not to look excited. He just sat in the back of the wagon with his feet hanging down, all the time thinking about what had happened with him and Mary Jane.

Soon the wagon pulled up in front of the big red barn and Josh's folks got off, leaving Josh to pull the horses around back with the other wagons. Josh found a place in back and unhooked the team. He took the bridles off each horse in turn and replaced them with a halter.

When he had finished staking the horses out, he placed a feedbag on each, then walked over to the back door of the barn. Josh stood there a moment, taking out a handkerchief to wipe the dust off his boots. That finished, he walked through the door.

Immediately he saw Mary Jane over in one corner, surrounded by several boys. Josh noticed that for someone with such a bad reputation, Mary Jane sure attracted attention. A feeling of jealousy momentarily flooded over him. He was standing there looking at her when someone grabbed him by the arm. It was Henry.

"Ma wants you, Josh. She's over there by the cake table."

"What she want?" Josh was annoyed at having to stop watching Mary Jane, but he made sure it didn't show on his face for fear his mother might suspect what they'd done.

"I don't know. Just told me to come and find you, that's all." Josh looked toward where his ma was sitting with some of the other women. She smiled and gestured him over.

"Josh, I want you to meet someone," she said, motioning to a girl standing beside her. "Carolyn, this is my son, Josh." Josh looked down at the girl Ma was talking to.

She was a mere slip of a girl, hardly coming up to Josh's chest. Carolyn's eyes were large for her head, making her look somewhat like a cow. The little twist of brown hair slipping over her forehead added to the picture. Josh tried not to think of her that way, but every time he looked at her she reminded him of old Alice, the family's milk cow. He had a funny thought and let his eyes drop down slightly, wondering if the picture would hold true. No such luck. She might as well be a boy in a dress--a boy with big cow-like eyes and a flat chest.

Josh almost laughed out loud but caught himself just in time. Carolyn didn't seem to notice, and it bothered Josh that he was having such thoughts. He blushed in embarrassment. It wasn't like him to make fun of others.

“Why don’t you ask her to dance, Josh?” his mother whispered when the girl wasn’t looking.

The last thing in the world Josh wanted to do right now was to dance. He always felt self-conscious in front of people. He was tall, even taller than most of the men, and stood out in crowds. Josh was about to politely refuse when he noticed that Mary Jane was dancing with Jack Redding, a boy he had gotten into a fist fight with at school the year before.

Jack was a bully, and although shorter than Josh, had deliberately picked a fight with him by calling him a "Big Ape" or something to that effect. Josh couldn't remember and it didn't really matter anyway, he had knocked the Redding boy down.

Ever since the fight, Jack had been going behind Josh's back telling lies about him. Josh let it ride. Now as Josh watched Mary Jane dancing with him, he began to get a little hot under the collar. He hardly noticed his ma talking to him.

"Why don't you kids go and dance together?” she asked again. “Josh, you can show Carolyn those steps I taught you last week. Josh, did you hear what I said? Are you feeling all right? You're not sick, are you, son?"

Josh turned back to his ma. "I'm sorry. I saw someone I wanted to talk to and was trying to see where they went."

"Well, aren't you going to ask Carolyn to dance?"

A thought suddenly came to Josh. "Miss Carolyn, do you want to dance?"

"I was hoping you would ask me," she said in a voice that had the strange effect of sounding like a cow mooing, completing the picture Josh had in his mind. With that she took Josh's hand and they walked to the dance floor.

As Josh looked around Mary Jane was nowhere to be seen. This really agitated him. Here he was, out on the dance floor making an idiot of himself in front of everybody, and she wasn't even watching. In fact, she wasn't anywhere to be found. As soon as the music stopped, Josh excused himself from Carolyn, giving an excuse that he had to remove the feedbags from the horses. After looking around for Mary Jane, he went outside to get some air. As long as he was outside, he thought he had really better go take the feedbags off the horses.

Walking outside he saw something small and white on the ground alongside one of the wagons. When he bent over to pick it up, he heard a sound coming from within the wagon a few feet away. It was dark except for the pale light of the full moon and there was no one else around except Josh, so he quietly edged up to the wagon to see what the noise was.

He cautiously peered over the side of the wagon and there to his dismay, was Mary Jane and Jack Redding lying on some blankets. Jack's hand was under Mary Jane's dress. Mary Jane had her head thrown back, with her blond hair wrapped around her neck in a kind of pigtail. Her eyes were closed, but the smile on her face showed full well that she was enjoying whatever it was Jack was doing to her. Josh couldn't believe what he was seeing. It was one thing to be immodest in the back of a barn, but here in full view of anyone that came along.

Since that day in the barn, Josh had thought of Mary Jane as someone special. He knew that not many people judged her to be any good, but Josh was young and hadn't really thought ahead to what people would think of him also. After all, Mary Jane was the first and only girl Josh had known. He hadn't even kissed a girl before, and now this.

The pain went deep in his heart. Quietly as he had come, Josh left them in their lust, only stopping by the corner of the barn to take one last look in their direction. There were tears in his eyes.

Josh had, for some time, toyed with the idea of running away and joining his older brothers in the Army, but had given up on the idea when Mary Jane and him had their affair in the barn--if you could call it an affair. It was more like the teacher instructing a pupil in the ways of life.

Josh was a fast learner and was ready for the next lesson a few minutes after he received the first one. But now his teacher was unwilling to teach him anymore, or worse, she was ready and willing to teach every other male anytime, anywhere. That hurt Josh even more. It wasn't fair for her to dangle a carrot in front of him only to snatch it away in such a short time.

The more Josh thought about it the madder he got, and when Josh got mad he did stupid things, and he was about to do something foolish now. It occurred to him again that the Army was trying to find men, and they weren't too choosy who they took. After all, he was as tall as many of the men around these parts and he could lie about his age if asked. His two older brothers, Sam and James, had both gone off to fight in the Civil War. Just because he was a little younger, why should that stop him? And now that Mary Jane had dumped him for every other male she could entice, there wouldn't be a better time to join up. Let her play with the boys. He was a man and he'd prove it.

With everybody for miles around at the barn dance, there wouldn't be a better time to slip away. These celebrations went on all night, so it would be at least twelve hours before his folks missed him and by then, he would be joined up and on his way to fight the war.

There wasn't anything here to stick around for, certainly not Mary Jane. Now that his mind was made up, Josh strolled over to where his ma was sitting talking to some women.

"Ma, can I talk to you a minute?"

"Yes, son." She stood up and walked with Josh to a quieter spot. Josh noticed his pa at the punch bowl again.

"Ma, do you mind if I stay here tonight? I'll catch a ride on home in the morning."

Ma looked at him for a long while. Josh wondered what she was thinking. Did she suspect what he was up to?

"Sure, Josh. I'm sure your pa won't mind. I'll feed the chickens for you so you can sleep in. Just try not to wake your pa when you come in. From the look of things he'll need to sleep a good one off." This was too good to be true, Josh thought.

"I'll sleep in the hayloft so he can sleep."

"That will be fine, Josh. I'll call you when supper's ready. You can sleep until then." Josh watched as his ma went back to where she had been sitting. He took a last, long look and walked out the door. Just as he came out of the barn, Jim Horner was passing by with his family.

"Mr. Horner! Could I get a ride with you as far as the fork in the road?"

"Why sure, Josh. Hop up here next to the flour sacks."

Josh thanked him, then sat down alongside the Horner kids. For a while they talked about all the things that had happened the last few months, then Josh settled down to think.

After he got off the wagon it was a short walk to the house. I'm going to have to be careful leaving here, he thought. With all the families coming home tonight I don't want to be seen. They might tell Pa which way I went.

Once in the house Josh quickly got a loaf of bread out of the bread drawer, added some dried meat, and rolled all of it up in brown paper. He started to take another shirt but decided he didn't need it. He thought about leaving a note but felt it would give him away. After changing into his everyday clothes, he put out into the night.

Now what way should I go? If I go to one of the towns close by I may be seen. He thought for a moment and decided to head for Louisville. It would take him all night to walk there. Once there it would be a simple matter to hop a freight going to one of the bigger cities where there was sure to be a recruiting station.

I'll be wearing blue within hours of getting on the train. Josh smiled at the thought. Every once in a while a dog would bark to mark Josh's passage in the night.

Off in the distance there came a light. At first Josh thought it was a lantern on someone's porch. But as Josh walked along, the light grew steadily brighter, much faster than it should for the pace Josh was maintaining.

Soon Josh could tell that the light was on some kind of wagon. He could just barely make out the outline. It seemed to have various pots and pans hung from its high wooden sides, and as it got closer he could hear the pans rattling against it. It made a terrible noise to Josh's sensitive hearing. How could anyone stand to ride in all that noise?

Josh looked around for some place to hide. About fifty feet away a big old oak stood, one of its branches hung low enough for Josh to grab and climb higher up the tree. A few moments later Josh was perched high enough to be out of sight when the wagon passed by. To his dismay, instead of continuing on down the road, the wagon pulled up under the very tree he was sitting in. Josh hugged the limb he was on so as not to move.

Maybe whoever's on the wagon just has to make a nature call, thought Josh. A barrel-chested man stepped down from the wagon, looked around, and then unloaded a small table and chair. He set the table down under the very limb Josh was on.

On the table the man placed a large pan with two notches in the rim, small holes along its side and four short legs on the bottom. In this he placed a small amount of kindling. On top of the kindling the man put several pieces of what to Josh looked like burnt wood.

That's a stupid thing to do, that burnt wood won't last long after he gets the fire going, thought Josh. Whoever heard of starting a fire in the middle of a table?

Josh continued to watch, all the time being careful not to give his position away. Soon the man had the fire going. Every few seconds he would blow on it and Josh would see the burnt wood glow red hot. Then Josh remembered how the blacksmith would do the same thing, but would use a bellows to bring the wood to a red glow instead of blowing on it as this man was doing. Was the man below him going to fix something with this fire? Then the man brought a freshly plucked chicken from the wagon and laid it on the table.

Before long the man reached into a box and brought out a long thin piece of metal. One end was pointed while the other end was bent into a crank. The man pierced the chicken with the sharp end, running it all the way through from chest to tail, then placing the ends of the rod into the notches in the pan.

Soon Josh could smell the food cooking. He was so hungry that it hurt to even look at the food below him. His stomach started to growl so Josh pulled himself closer to the tree hoping to quiet his stomach down. It worked, but made his stomach hurt. He hadn't eaten since the noon meal and it was now past midnight.

He thought about climbing down from his perch and asking the man for some of that chicken to eat, but knew he didn't dare. Josh was about to give in to his hunger when he heard several horses coming from out of the darkness.

In a matter of minutes the riders were upon the camp. Josh could see only two men, but knew there was at least one more holding back from the camp, possibly two. One man stepped down from his horse and walked directly toward the man cooking dinner.

"Hello," said the cook to the other. "What can I do for you gents?"

"Just stay put, mister! Keep your hands where I can see them!"

It was then Josh saw the reflection from the badge the rider wore on his chest. Must be the sheriff, thought Josh. I hope he's not looking for me.

The sheriff spoke again. "There were two of you in town yesterday. Where's your sidekick? We come to take the both of you in."

"What for, sheriff? I'm just a peaceful peddler of pots and pans."

"Sure you are. That's why you killed Miss Josie. She wouldn't buy anything from you, right?"

"Sheriff, I ain't killed nobody in all my life!"

"Then it was your partner! Where is he? You might as well tell here and now. There's no tellin' what might happen to you when we get you to town." The peddler shot a look toward the sheriff but said nothing.

"Miss Josie was well liked and we're not going to let you or your partner get away with it," the sheriff said.

The peddler kept on cooking his meal, but Josh could see that he was slowly moving around the table towards a pile of rags he had placed there earlier. Inch by inch, the man's right hand moved closer to the rags.

"You don't mind if I wipe my hands off do you, sheriff? Then I'll tell you what you want to know."

The sheriff gave the man a hard look, suspicion showing in his face, but the man at the table didn't catch it. "Go ahead. But I'm warning you, no funny stuff."

The peddler picked up a rag from the top of the pile and started wiping his hands. "Sure do get grease all over when you cook a chicken this way." He threw the first rag on the ground, and then casually reached for another one.

At that moment Josh saw what the man was really reaching for. Buried in the pile he could see the butt of a Colt .44. Before Josh could warn the sheriff, the man jerked the gun out. He was bringing the barrel in line with the sheriff when a two-foot chunk of oak caught the peddler in the side of the head, knocking him to the ground. In an instant the sheriff was on him, kicking the Colt away at the same time.

"Thanks Jake. I didn't catch what he was up to. We ought to string him up right here, but I don't think the townspeople would like missing the hanging. Besides, I still want to find out where the other one went."

The thought occurred to Josh that if anyone saw him up in the tree, they would just naturally figure he was the other one they were looking for. Now he knew how a coon felt when treed by a pack of hounds. Here he was, a runaway, stuck on a tree limb, about to get hanged all in less than five hours. Josh almost laughed at the thought of it all, but decided he didn't want it to be his last laugh. At that very moment he noticed the brown paper package with the loaf of bread and meat was almost ready to fall from his pocket. He froze, praying for all that he was worth that it wouldn't fall while at the same time knowing he was powerless to stop it.

The men below had finished tying the peddler up. They placed the peddler across the back of his own horse and ran a rope under its belly, tying one end to the man's hands and the other to his feet.

"Just want to make sure you don't get lost before we get you back to town," said the man who was doing the tying. "Is that too tight for you?'

"Yeah, it's cutting into my arms."

"Is that right? Well, I'll just have to see what I can do about that." With that, the man pulled the rope even tighter around the peddler's wrist. The peddler knew enough not to say any more for fear of having the ropes pulled even tighter.

"You about done, Jake?" the sheriff asked.

"He won't be going anywhere by himself, I've seen to that! What you want done with his things? It's a cinch he won't need them any more."

"Just leave them tonight. That way if the other fellow is anywhere around, he'll probably take off with the wagon. We'll be able to catch him by next evening, just like we caught this one tonight."

"You might be right. You can't hide a thing like that just anywhere," the third man said while eyeing the cooking chicken. "That chicken smells mighty good. Can't we help ourselves to some?"

"I heard tell this fellow poisoned a whole posse once with a chicken just like the one he's got cookin' there," Jake said.

The hungry man looked Jake straight in the eye, trying to figure out if he was kidding about the chicken.

"Yep, as I recall it was just over a year ago, killed them all to the man. I don't know how he could have got wind of us coming, but just in case I'd be mighty careful." Jake looked back at the man, unable to meet his gaze for more than a second.

"That's easy for you to say. You were just done eating when we come to get you for this business we're on."

"Maybe so, but I'd not take a chance with anything this fellow cooked. Come on, you can get something in town when we get back. If we get going it should only take us a few hours to get there." Jake wheeled his horse around toward town.

"He might be right." It was the sheriff talking this time. "Why take the chance? You got a family that needs you alive, not poisoned by some chicken you couldn't keep your hands off."

"All right! Give me a chance to cinch my saddle and I'll be right with you." The sheriff gave him an unbelieving look. "You can get going and I'll be along in a minute," the hungry man said, angrily. The sheriff shook his head, and then rode out with Jake and the prisoner in tow.

The deputy waited for them to fade into the night, before walking over to the bird roasting over the spit. He carefully took the meat off the fire and pulled it close to his nose.

"Smells all right," he said aloud to himself. The deputy started to take a bite then stopped, looked the bird over then placed it back on the fire. "Let the damn thing burn!" he said in disgust.

He climbed on his horse and started to leave when to Josh's horror the package of bread fell from his pocket and hit the table below. The deputy wheeled his mount around at the noise, his gun drawn. Josh froze, not even daring to breathe. After a few moments of straining to hear, the deputy turned his horse back around and headed into the night. "I'm getting too old for this!" Josh heard him say as he rode away into the darkness.

Josh was exhausted. The whole episode lasted only ten minutes but to Josh it seemed like the longest ten minutes of his life. He started to climb down from the tree, then hesitated. What if they came back for something? Maybe they figured by staying just out of sight they could catch the peddler's friend.

I can't stay in this tree all night, and that chicken looks mighty good, Josh thought. He knew the chicken wasn't poisoned. He'd seen the peddler's surprise when the men approached earlier. That chicken was as good as any, and if Josh could get to it safely he'd take little time putting it in his belly.

A noise caught his attention. It wasn't close, but it made him take notice. He listened to try to make out what it was. Sound can travel for a mile or more out here in the open. This time the sound came clearer to his ears. It was one man trying to find another in the dark. Yes, that's what it was. He was sure now. He recognized the voice of the sheriff. The hungry man was trying to catch up in the dark and had lost his way. The sheriff was trying to direct him to where he was.

Josh dropped to the ground, pulled the chicken off the spit and headed out, eating as he went.

Chapter III

Josh hit Louisville just after sunup with a full stomach of roasted chicken. A crowd of people was disbanding further up the street at what must be the town square. Every town had one, a place where speeches were made and other public events held.

"What's all the excitement?" Josh asked a man walking past.

"Go see for yourself if you got the belly for it!" the man said.

Josh walked to where the crowd had been. There were still enough people to make Josh have to push his way through. Even though Josh was taller than most of the others, he was unable to see anything in front of them. He was just a few people from the front when he got his first sight of what they were looking at.

There impaled on sticks were two heads. The first head was that of the peddler whom Josh had seen during the night. The second was that of a younger man not much older than Josh. At first Josh wanted to puke, then after taking a deep breath, curiosity got the best of him.

"What happened to these men?" Josh asked a lady standing beside him.

"They's murderers! They raped and killed Miss Josie two nights back. The posse brought 'em back last night. We hanged 'em at daybreak."

Josh couldn't believe they would hang a man without a trial, let alone cut his head off and put it on a stick, but there they were for all to see. While standing amongst the crowd, Josh saw a man come over and spit on the faces of the dead men.

"Why did you do that, mister?" Josh asked. The man looked Josh over from head to foot.

"You're not from around here, are you, boy?"

"No, sir, I've come to catch a train so I can enlist in the Union Army."

"Well, I'll tell you, boy. Josie was my daughter." The man started to break down and cry. "What these two got was too good for them!" The man sobbed as he turned and left without looking back.

Another man standing in back of Josh said, "He's right, you know. We should have cut their heads off before we hanged 'em."

Before Josh realized what he was saying, he asked the man, "Who did cut off their heads?"

"Why no one, boy! The hangman does that!"

"I don't understand how you mean, mister."

"You see, boy, he ties the noose with thirteen coils and then places them behind the condemned man's right ear. Then he cinches the rope up tight--not so tight so as to choke them to death, mind you. We wouldn't want them to die before we hanged them, would we, boy?"

"I guess not, sir."

The man began again. "The hangman then goes down below them to be hanged, and ties a sack of dirt or whatever else is handy to their feet. You with me, boy?"

"Yes, sir."

"The rope from their feet to the sack has a knot tied in it. The knot remains over a notch in the trap door while the sack remains under the door. The rope is very short and by placing the knot above the trap, the sack is supported by the door, not their legs. You got that so far, boy?"

"Yes, sir, I think so."

"Anyhow, when the hangman pulls the lever, the trap door springs open and the sacks fall with all the weight in them, jerks the condemned man's body down hard through the trap door opening. Some hangmen can snap a man's head off the very first try! This one sure did. What a sight it was. Now you know how it's done. Just make sure you don't get on the wrong end of a rope. It could ruin your whole day."

That could have been me on the second pole, Josh thought to himself. If any of the men had seen me up on the tree, they just naturally would have thought I was his partner. And I wouldn't be standing here now. A chill went up his spine and the air felt very cold.

The train whistle sounded and Josh got set to hop on board. As he stood there, he realized that he didn't know how to hop a freight. When he was younger, his grandpa had told him stories about the hoboes and how they hitched rides on the rails. If only he could remember how his grandfather said they got on without getting their heads beat in by the yard bosses that regularly patrolled the freight yards.

Didn't seem to be anybody around. Maybe all those stories were just that--stories. After all, who would care if anybody caught a ride on one of the empty boxcars?

Josh caught sight of a small man hurrying along the tracks toward the train that Josh himself wanted to catch. Josh figured he'd just wait and see what happens. If there's anything to those stories that Grandpa told, I should see somebody come along shortly to take the man off the train. Josh waited, nothing happened. But still Josh wasn't able to get those stories out of his mind. The small man disappeared from view behind an old shed that stood between Josh and the tracks.

Did he hear a man scream? He turned his head in the direction the sound had come from. He could hear nothing more. Must have been something from the train's engine making the noise. Still, he wasn't sure. The engine started to move, very slowly at first, then gathered speed. Josh knew if he didn't make his move now, it might be hours before another train came along.

He grabbed for the small bundle of food he had wrapped in the brown paper, tucked it under his arm and started to run after the train. Ahead he could see the open door of a boxcar. Faster he ran. Now he was a few feet from the door. He reached for it--almost. Must run faster. Josh was now pacing the train. Can't look down . . . must concentrate on the handle . . . don't take my eyes off it . . . grab it--now! He threw his arm out towards the handle.

The log had been waiting for him several hundred feet up the track. One second Josh was about to jump on board the train, the next he was flying through the air, his arms seeking something, anything, to break his fall. There was nothing. Josh's head slammed into the hard loose gravel of the rail bed. He could feel it ripping at the skin of his hands as he tried to protect his face from injury. He lay there a long minute.

"Why would anyone leave a log laying around so close to the tracks?" Josh said aloud. He picked himself up. The train was almost out of sight. "Might as well eat something, no tellin' how long before another freight comes by." Josh started to walk back to the spot where earlier he had stood to watch the hobo. He wasn't paying attention; he was too busy trying to get the paper unwrapped so he could eat.

He had just placed a piece of bread in his mouth, when looking up to see where he was, that he noticed the log. Or was it a log? Josh took a long breath and swallowed the bread whole. The log he had tripped over wasn't a log at all.

It was a body--a dead body to be sure. Josh had no doubts about that. He bent down alongside the little hobo and gently rolled the old man over so he could see his face. His face. What face? The old hobo looked as though a mule had kicked him full in the front of his head.

Josh heard some loose gravel scatter across the roadbed a short distance away. "You're going to get the same as your friend!" the yard boss hollered.

He was a larger than normal-sized man. His skin was tanned the shade of leather. Red hair circled about his head contrasting his bald spot that was burned almost black from the sun. He looked mean, meaner than any man Josh had ever seen. Josh was big too, big for a boy, but he seemed small and fragile compared to the man that was bearing down on him.

In the yard boss' left hand he held a cut-off ax handle that was covered with blood. Josh had always been able to hold his own in a fight, but this man wasn't human. He was a demon--a paid killer hired by the railroad to keep nonpaying riders off the freights.

Before Josh could gain his balance the man had closed the distance between them to a few feet. Josh saw the blow coming. The man had telegraphed his intention before he struck, and Josh was able to roll out of the way.

Regaining his feet, he quickly headed for the only place that might shelter him from the man's savage attack--a lone outhouse a few yards away. Josh made it inside, pulling the door shut behind him.

Lucky for Josh the door had a rope strung through it to act as a sort of handle. Grabbing the rope with both hands, he pulled with all his might. With Josh holding most of the rope on the inside, there wasn't enough for the yard detective to grasp on the outside.

"It won't do you any good to hold up in there, kid. I'll cut the rope!" Josh looked around for something to protect himself with. There was nothing. Just the rope and a few pieces of paper.

Why didn't I just run? Maybe I could have outrun him, he thought. Through the cracks he could see the man's face flushed with anger. He could also hear him cutting through the rope on the outside.

The rope suddenly came loose in Josh's hands. He fell backward, almost sitting on the hole as if he were in there to relieve himself, instead of trying to save his life. He braced himself for the blow he knew was coming. The door flew open and there before him stood the menacing figure of the yard boss, ax handle posed for the final strike.

Unknown to the yard boss, another man had come up behind him. "I wouldn't do that if I were you," the man said in a low voice. "Just lower the club and turn around real slow. I mean real slow if you know what's good for you. That's my boy you're after."

Josh couldn't believe his ears. Was it really Pa? He tried to see but the hulk of the yard boss blocked his view.

The yard boss remained facing Josh. "I don't hear you talking, mister, so you just better be on your way. This here's a hobo. Saw him get off the train just this morning."

The man behind him placed a well aimed kick square in Red's back. Josh could see the pain spread across the man's face. Slowly his grip on the ax handle loosened and it fell from his grasp. He tried to say something, but couldn't find the wind to get it out.

John Templer kicked the man again. This time Josh could see his pa's face. It was calm, as if he were having a friendly chat with a neighbor.

"I said turn around or I'll kick you again. That's no hobo! That's my son, and I aim to take him home with me right now! Step aside or I'll hurt you some more." Josh had never heard his pa talk like this, let alone hurt anybody as he was doing to this man.

"He murdered a hobo. I saw the body!" Josh yelled to his pa. "He's a real bad one, Pa."

John stepped in close behind the man. He seemed to gather up strength, then threw a kidney punch to the murderer's right side. The killer's legs buckled under him. He started to slip to the ground.

Josh's pa grabbed the man's belt and held him from falling all the way.

"Get out of there, son. There's someone waiting to use it." Josh slipped past the half-conscious bully. John took a few steps forward and deposited the large red head down into the hole, giving one last punch to the man's kidney area.

"You should feel right at home in there, you bastard." He let the man's body slip to the floor, his head still caught in the hole.

"Get over to the wagon, son," John Templer told Josh as calmly as before. Josh started to walk past his pa when he heard a noise from behind him. It was the yard boss, with the ax handle raised overhead. Before Josh could react the ax came swinging down toward his pa's head with all the fury the man could muster. As if in slow motion Josh saw the ax coming down and the man's face behind it contorted from anger, and to his surprise, his pa's hand reached up and stopped the savage swing of the ax handle in midair.

For a brief second the two men faced each other, John Templer standing very calm and determined while the other man slowly came to the realization of what had just happened. John's right arm came up slowly and back while his hand made into a fist. Josh could hear bones break as his pa's fist slammed into the other man's face, first once, then twice, then a third time in quick succession. The redheaded brute staggered, blood pouring from his nose, and then ever so slowly turned on his heels. Again John Templer caught the man by his belt and crammed the man's head back down the outhouse hole.

"Best stay there this time!" John Templer ordered as he walked away. The brute's body shuddered once then went still.

Now that Josh was safe, the realization that his pa had found him and saved him sunk in. Out of the fire and into the pan, thought Josh. He knew that his time of reckoning would be soon at hand.

"Get on the wagon, boy. We still got something to do." Josh obeyed without replying. He knew better than to provoke his pa right now. Funny, Pa hadn't said anything about Josh running away yet. Josh knew his pa must be boiling under the collar. It would just take time before he blew. Josh took another look in the direction of the outhouse. From where he sat, all he could see was a pair of legs. They didn't move.

Pa turned the horses toward the east end of town. Home was west of town, about 20 miles. Josh wondered where Pa was heading. Soon he pulled the team over in front of a small wood frame building. Josh noticed someone had built an addition onto the building out of brick. He also saw there were bars on the single window.

The sign over the door read "Sheriff's Office." Pa didn't bother to get down. "Hey, in there! Come on out here!" The door opened with a start.

"What you hollerin' about?" The man had been napping inside, and was now rubbing the sleep from his eyes. He was the same man Josh saw out at the peddler's wagon. "I asked you what all the commotion's about. You gonna tell me or do I have to guess?"

John Templer looked the sheriff straight in the eye. The sheriff tried to stare back but was forced to look away. Templer never spoke. Finally the sheriff said, “What can I do for you gents?”

"I left you something down in the outhouse by the tracks. You can see his handiwork a few yards away." The sheriff's mouth dropped open. "He tried to do the same with the boy!"

"Do what?" the sheriff wanted to know.

"Killed somebody with an ax handle! The corpse is lying close by. The killer's taking a rest in the outhouse. That's all I got to say!" John Templer started to rein the horses around toward home.

"Wait up there, fella. I ain't done with you yet! If what you say is true, I'll need you for the trial."

"It's true, but I don't have time for any trial. Didn't see him do it anyway." The sheriff started to demand they stay but thought better of it.

"Once you get down there, won't be hard for you to put it together. So long, sheriff." John Templer slapped the rear of the horses with the reins. In a few minutes they were out of town.

Pa looked over at Josh but didn't say anything. What's he up to, Josh wondered.

"You look a little pale, boy. Better crawl back on the feed sacks and catch a few hour's sleep. We'll talk when you wake up." The thought crossed Josh's mind, “Wish I could sleep for about ten years.” He began to sweat.

Chapter IV

Josh's face felt hot. He had been sleeping close to four hours, and the sun was now high overhead. Josh opened his eyes slowly, first looking toward the wagon seat to see if Pa was still there knowing that he probably wouldn't be, as the wagon had stopped moving. The last thing Josh wanted to do was bring attention to himself before he had a chance to gather his thoughts.

Josh carefully rolled onto his side, so he could see his pa through the crack between the sideboards. His pa was bending over a small fire he had built holding the old coffee pot he used while traveling in his left hand. His shirt was pulled taut, revealing a back as strong as any man's Josh could remember seeing. Funny, he hadn't noticed before how strong his father was.

Maybe I can go back to sleep and put the punishment off, Josh mused. No, he had better take it now and get it over with. No use waiting until he got home. Pa would only have more time to fume about everything, and it would be all the worse for Josh.

"Come over here, son. I hear you stirring." Josh had no choice but to get up now. "You must be starved. You hardly took enough with you to feed an ant."

"I'm pretty hungry," Josh agreed.

"I've got some grub cookin' that will fill you up. Bring a couple of tin plates over here and get it dished up for us." Josh started loosening the strap on the travel box. "Put your hat on while you're at it. You got a bad burn from sleepin' with your face uncovered."

Josh didn't need to be told he was sunburned. His face felt on fire, but the sunburn didn't bother him half as much as what he knew his dad had in store for him later. Finding the plates, he walked over and started filling them with succotash. His pa still hadn't turned to face him.

"Put mine over there on the log. I'll get it in a bit, after I get this coffee boiled up." Josh moved around the fire. Pa looked down at the flames, his broad-brimmed hat hiding his eyes from Josh.

"Aren't you going to eat before it gets cold, pa?"

"Josh," John Templer spoke in almost a murmur, "I want to get something off my chest and here's as good a place as any."

Josh stiffened. "I know what I did was wrong, Pa, but--"

Pa stopped him with a wave of the hand. "Just listen to what I've got to say, son." He still stared at the fire from under his hat brim.

"When your ma woke me to tell me you weren't in the barn, it didn't surprise me at all. I've been expecting it for some time. I could see it in your eyes. I just didn't know when you'd take off." Josh was shocked at finding out his pa had been expecting him to run away.

"At first, I wanted to find you and beat the tar out of you. Then the more I thought about it, the more I realized how hard the war must be on you. Everywhere a person goes these days people are talking about how the battles are going. We're not the only family who has sons off to fight. Just the other day Ed Johnson got news of his son being wounded just outside of Vicksburg." Pa's voice seemed sad as he spoke.

"All this talk, and you being bigger than most men, but too young to go off and fight for your country. You are of my own blood. Heaven knows if it weren't for your ma and you two boys I'd be right there with your brothers giving it to them Rebs! So you see, Josh?" Pa looked up at him. There were tears in his eyes as he spoke again. "I can't blame you for running away. Your ma and I love you. We want you to come home."

"I'm sorry, Pa. I really want to come home before I get myself into any more trouble."

Pa nodded his head. A little smile spread across his face. "Let's eat. I haven't filled my belly since leaving the barn dance."

Josh looked at his pa and felt a closeness he hadn't felt before. "Let's hurry so we can get on home," Josh said. "I got some chores that need to be done."

"All right, boy. Let's load up the wagon and get home for some real home cookin'. Why there's just enough here for a good snack before dinner."

"Pa?" Josh asked. "Where did you learn to fight like that? I knew you could punch hard. I've felt it enough when we're playing around, but you never told me that you could put someone down like you did this morning."

"I guess I learned how back when I was living in Chicago. There were always gangs of kids roaming the streets. You learned how to fight or you'd have your head kicked in." Pa looked off into space for a moment while remembering some far off scene in his mind, a scene far off in both time and distance.

"Bad place to grow up," he said. "Boy, was I glad when we moved away from there. My pa got sent out here to run a crew of Gandy Dancers working on the railroad. They would have to do all the repair work for a hundred miles on either side of town."

Pa took a bite of his food. "When you were just a baby, my pa would tell you all about the hoboes that rode the rails. That's why I figured you'd head this way. It's the only rail line coming anywhere near our place."

Josh looked at his pa. "I guess I was pretty stupid, wasn't I?"

"You might say so, but wisdom will come with age. Just look how smart I am." They both roared at that.

Josh couldn't remember when he had felt this good. Twice in twenty-four hours he had cheated death. First, when the sheriff had come for the peddler, and again when he was trapped in the outhouse. Now with his belly full and a soft breeze blowing in his hair, he was going back home with Pa.

Best of all, Pa wasn't even mad at him for running away. Josh reasoned that if he couldn't make it on his own for a day, how was he going to make it in the Army facing the enemy? Boy, did he have some things to learn.

Josh didn't care how many heroes came home from the war. He knew it would be a long time before he went traipsing through the countryside by himself. He had learned a valuable lesson: never let your emotions overrule your head. It would be a lesson Josh would rarely forget.

"Looks like we're going to get some wind when the sun goes down from the look of that sky," Pa said as they rode along. "Might be gettin' a bit nippy." Pa reached down behind the wagon seat and got a bottle of moonshine he kept stashed there for just such a night as this.

"Uncork this for me, son. I need a little nip to take the chill off." Josh took the jug from pa's hand and pulled the cork free.

"Go ahead and take a swig, son. It'll warm your insides."

"You sure, Pa? Ma doesn't want any of us boys drinking. She'll be awful mad when she smells the spirits on my breath."

"Well, I think she'll understand this time. She was real scared I wouldn't find you. Go ahead, Josh. Take a pull on that jug but save some for me."

They rode on, each taking a turn at the jug. It was after midnight when they arrived home. The horses came to a stop in front of the barn. Pa and Josh were fast asleep in the back of the wagon, dead to the world. The empty jug lay between them.

Chapter V

The last warm days of October had slipped by unnoticed. One day it was warm and you had only to wear a light shirt and pants to be comfortable. The next day there was a chill in the air that had the unmistakable feeling of winter.

It had been several weeks since Josh had come back home. Now as he did his chores around the farm, he was glad he wasn't out in the cold fighting a battle in some unknown place. At times like these he often wondered where his brothers were and if they were all right.

A letter would trickle in once in a while from one of them. Ma would gather the rest of the family around her and read it carefully out loud. The letters would always be full of hope that the war would end soon, with some of the highlights of a battle or two fought by the writer. There would also be an air of sadness about the letter, and it would always arrive months after they were written, so you never knew if the sender was alive, or dead.

After reading it, Ruth would hold it close to her bosom as though it were her son himself she was holding. John would look over at her, not saying anything. Josh knew his folks didn't have to talk; they were both thinking the same thing and needed time to be alone.

"Come on, Henry, it's about high time we cleaned out the stalls in the barn," Josh would say. He never had to tell Henry twice on these occasions. He, too, understood their need to be alone.

One day as Josh was out milking the cow, he heard a wagon drive up in front of the house. He wanted to stop milking and go see who it was, but since Alice was a skittish animal he figured he better not stop until he was done. It seemed to take hours to finish the milking. Finally done, Josh hurried into the house to see who the company was.

"Wipe your feet, Josh. You're tracking mud everywhere." Josh looked down at his feet. His boots were covered with dirt and manure from the barn.

"Sorry, Ma. I got in a hurry to see who was here." He tiptoed out to clean his boots, but not before he saw that the visitors were Ed Johnson and his boy

Dave. After hurriedly cleaning the mud off, he went back in to see Dave and hear about his exploits in the War. Dave was only two years older than Josh, but it was two years that made all the difference in who went and who stayed.

"Hi, Josh, long time no see. How ya been?"

Josh didn't want to talk about himself. He was hungry to hear about the war. "I'm all right. What about yourself?" Josh saw that Dave had his jacket pulled around him as if he were cold.

"I'm home. I guess that's all that counts, at least that's what everyone's been tellin' me." Josh could hear an edge to Dave's voice.

"You got yourself wounded I hear. How bad?"

Mr. Johnson turned his head toward Josh and gave him a look as to say, "Don't ask!" It was too late. Dave started to say something, but before he could talk, he burst out in tears. Josh didn't know what to do.

"I didn't mean no harm, Mr. Johnson. I just thought Dave would want to tell me all about the army and how he got wounded."

Dave got hold of himself. "It's all right! I'm better now." Josh felt awful at having made his friend upset.

"Josh, can we go outside and talk? "I've got something to show you."

"Sure, Dave, if that's what you want." Dave motioned Josh to the door, then followed him out. Once outside, the two boys walked out to the corral.

"What was it you wanted to tell me, Dave?"

"Just give me a minute. I'm not quite ready yet. What have you been doing while I was gone?" Josh thought about telling Dave about Mary Jane, then thought better of it.

"I tried running away to join up, but only made it over to Louisville. Almost got myself killed, too!"

Dave didn't look at Josh; he just kept looking off in the distance. "How'd you almost get killed by running away?"

Josh told all about the peddler and the yard boss and still Dave looked off into space. Finally Josh's curiosity got the best of him. "Dave, what's wrong? Are you sick? You keep that jacket all wrapped around you like you're cold. It doesn't seem that cold to me."

Dave turned around and faced Josh. "No, I'm not cold. It's just that I don't want anyone to see my wound."

Josh looked at his friend. "How bad is it?"

Dave looked down. "It's pretty bad. That's why I hide it. You see, Josh, I got hit with some grape shot in my right arm."

Josh put his hand on the shoulder of his friend. "Lots of men got shot. It's not so bad. Why, give you another couple of weeks and we'll be out squirrel hunting just as though nothing ever happened."

"I doubt that, Josh." Dave let his coat fall to the ground. Josh could not believe what he saw. He was totally shocked. Before him stood Dave with only one arm. His right arm had been severed just below the shoulder. A bloodstained rag was wrapped tightly around it. Josh could see dark blood oozing from the end of Dave's stump. He felt sick. He was going to throw up. Dave pulled the jacket back across his shoulders.

"When I joined up I thought it was going to be fun, a new uniform and a .60 caliber musket. I was one of the men. Now I'm only half a man, and for what? Tears welled up in Dave's eyes.

"It was terrible out there. Every night as I went to sleep, I wondered if tomorrow would be my last day alive. Then we got in a battle just east of Vicksburg.

"I had just killed a man! He wasn't much older than you, Josh. I took careful aim. As I pulled the trigger I could see the bullet hit. He was knocked clean off his feet. He just sat there where he had fallen. He looked at me till he died." There was pain in Dave's voice.

"That's when the grape shot got me. It was a few minutes before I even knew I was hit. Then the pain came; it hurt something awful."

"Come on, Dave. I'll help you to the house." Josh's voice was trembling. And I was going to join the army and come home a hero, Josh thought in disgust. Dave was one of those heroes. But no one was cheering, for Dave was soon to die. Gangrene was slowly setting in his wound.

One week later, David Johnson lay in a pine box in the little church on the hill outside of town. For Dave there would be no tomorrow. The war had not only taken his arm, but his life too. For the people around Josh's home, David's death brought home fears they had all lived with since the war began. Now those fears took on an even greater meaning. How many more loved ones would they lose before it ended? Josh prayed that his brothers would not be as unlucky as David.

The whole community turned out to pay their last respects to the Johnson boy. Even the Horsteads were there. Mary Jane, whom Josh hadn't seen in several months, was standing just outside the circle of people gathered around the grave. Josh noticed she had put on a little weight. He also noticed she watched his every move. It made him feel uneasy with her being there, an uneasiness that would grow with time. But for now, Josh would just ignore her.

The journey home was a sad one for Josh. He and Dave had practically grown up together. Now Dave was dead. Josh sat in the back of the wagon with his feet dangling down. He watched as the church got smaller and smaller in the distance. He had held back the tears throughout the funeral. Now he could hold them back no more. He silently wept for his friend Dave.

The days were shorter now and Josh had fewer chores to do. The news going around said that the war would end any week now. There was an air of excitement. Mothers and wives were making ready for their sons and husbands to return.

After a few weeks of waiting for more news, people began to worry. Was it just another rumor, or was there some truth to it? Was the war soon to be over? Josh's family waited, too. For a month they had no new information, no mail--nothing. The cold winds of November and the snows of December made it impossible to get the mails that were slow, at best, through.

One day in late December, Pa took the sled into town for some much needed supplies and a few Christmas gifts. He and Ma had prayed their family would all be home to celebrate Christmas together. Such was not to be. The war still raged on with no end in sight.

While in town Pa heard one piece of rumor that he thought might be of interest to Ma. Someone had mentioned that the Horstead girl was looking more than a little plump around the middle and it wasn't from overeating.

When Ruth heard the news she threw her hands up and exclaimed, "Oh, that girl! She'll bring trouble down on some unsuspecting family for sure. I don't reckon she even knows who the father is."

"One thing's for sure," interrupted Pa, "her old man will make the best of it at somebody else's loss, that's for sure."

"Well, she can't blame any of our boys, with the older ones off to war and Henry and Josh being as young as they are," said Ma. "Not that they wouldn't want to pin it on someone with land and a little money."

Henry came in the door. "Got my chores done, Pa. Can I see what you brung from town?"

Ma looked over at her husband. "We'll discuss this after dinner when we're alone."

Pa watched his wife as she busied herself setting the table. "I checked for mail today--nothing. Ben said not to be expecting any till the snow clears. They're using all the trains to supply the soldiers, trying to break Lees back before summer."

Ruth turned to face John. "We've all heard that before. I pray it's true this time."

"I know what you mean."

"If only our boys could come home before Christmas. I'd never ask God for anything ever again!"

Christmas came on the winds of another storm, but nothing was heard of Samuel or James. Soon a new year arrived to take the place of the old. The war was over!

All the fighting, the killing, the insaneness of it all was ended. Stopped in its insidious tracks, as though someone, somewhere pulled a single lever and brought the murderous machine to a halt.

The news went throughout the country like wildfire. The war was over! Families could be unified again. The Union had won! The slaves were free!

The South was there for the carpetbaggers to ransack and loot. Once noble Southern families were ruined, destroyed by the madness of it all. The year 1865 would live in the minds of Americans forever. The bloodiest conflict known to modern man had come to a close.

The Templers were hardly prepared for the ending of the war. Like most families they had hoped for the end. But when it finally came, it came as a shock.

Now another fear crept into their lives. They hadn't received any mail from their boys for a long time, since the early part of November, and the letter they had received was over two months old at the time they got it. It was from Samuel, and since Sam was in the cavalry and James in the artillery, the letter had no mention of the whereabouts of James. The letter did say, however, that at the time of its writing Sam was on his way to Vicksburg, a place that saw many bloody skirmishes between the Blue and the Gray.

It was now April and Lee had surrendered. The volunteer troops were the first to be mustered out. Then the soldiers whose enlistment had been prolonged by the war were paid off. These veterans spread out through the countryside like rabbits scurrying for cover.

Some wore their full uniforms. Others wore only fragments of uniforms--pants, hats, maybe a jacket or shirt--most dirty from weeks, even months, of wearing without being washed. Some were so dirty you couldn't tell the color of them from even a few feet away.

When Josh would see a lone figure approaching on foot from afar, he would first let his folks know, then holler a greeting to the stranger. Ma would come out with a small loaf of bread and some hot tea. While the stranger ate, Pa would ply him for news of Samuel or James. When none was forthcoming they would offer the man the use of their barn and some fresh hay to sleep the night in.

One day in the latter part of April with the clouds laying low against the hills, it began to rain. Not a patch of blue shone all morning. A moderate wind blew, forcing the cows and horses to turn their backs to the wind. There was an air of doom hanging about the countryside. Josh felt down in the mouth, not knowing whether it was him or the weather.

Upon waking, he immediately stepped out of bed only to find the cat directly under his foot. It let out a yowl and turned on the bare foot that had stepped on it. Before Josh could get his foot away, the cat had left it streaked with blood. Josh started to let out a string of cuss words, then held back for fear his mother would hear him.

"I'll get you later!" Josh half yelled, while shaking his fist at the scrambling feline. He sat back on the bed examining his wounded foot. "Darn that cat anyhow! I'll probably get the mange and all the hair will fall off my leg." Josh laughed at the thought.

After getting dressed, including his rain slicker, he started out for the barn and his chores. No sooner had he opened the door than he was faced by the same cat that had attacked him earlier. With one swift kick the cat went flying head over teakettle out to the mud.

"I told you, I'd get you cat!" Josh said. And with that he headed out to find Alice.

The rain turned the barnyard to mush, and with each step he would have to reach down and pull his boots back on. After slipping in the mud, he had pulled his foot completely out of his boot. He tried to balance on one foot while putting the other boot on. He had just gotten his other boot pulled out of the mud and was about to put it on when he heard a snorting behind him. With a splash the boot went one way and his foot, missing the boot altogether, went deep into the muddy slime.

"Looks like you would be better off with bare feet, boy!" The voice startled Josh to attention. But when he stood up he was thrown off balance again. This time he landed flat on his back, going deep enough in the mud so that it came clear around him. There wasn't any place he wasn't covered with slop.

Josh flung the mixture off his right hand so as to be able to wipe his face clean enough to see. He let the rain clear his eyes so that he could look at the owner of the voice. Above him, mounted on a great black horse rode a bearded man with a long saber in his right hand. The soldier wore the uniform of a Union cavalry officer.

"Well, boy, you gonna roll over just to finish the job, or are you going to get up so I can see how tall you are?" Josh didn't move; he just looked up at the officer. Something about the face--familiar, yet hard and strange, as if it was someone he had met once but couldn't remember the name.

"Is that a new way of milking the cows I haven't seen before? I know I've been gone a long time but I didn't think things would change that much, kid!" Josh took another wipe at his face, this time spreading more mud across it. He spit some out of this mouth.

"How do you know my name, stranger?" Josh wanted to know.

"Stranger, is it now? I would think you might still remember my name, although I have changed some I reckin'." Josh got to his knees then slowly struggled to his feet. He no longer cared that he only had one boot on.

"Sam? Is it you, brother? Ma! Pa! Sam's home!" In the excitement Sam's great black stallion skidded to the side. Sam, who wasn't expecting the sudden sideward movement, had been leaning over to one side while talking to Josh. In a second he was like a great bald eagle, wings outstretched, deposited alongside Josh in the barnyard ooze. Josh reached down to help his big brother up.

"Going to help me milk, are you, Sam?"

Both boys hugged each other. Pa who had seen the rider from inside the house, ran across the yard, and with one mighty jump cleared the fence and landed feet first beside his two sons. The instant his feet touched the scum, they went out from each other. In less than a second he was sitting up to his belt in the mud and manure. Undaunted, he grabbed Sam by the waist and hung on until Sam was again pulled off his feet.

By now Ruth stood on the front porch trying to decide what was happening with her men folk. To her it looked like John and Josh were attacking a stranger while a black horse stood by watching. Henry just stood there beside his mother with his mouth open as usual. Finally, Pa waved his wife over.

“It’s Samuel!” he shouted. “It’s our boy!”

Ruth picked up her skirts and ran faster than Josh had ever seen her run, only stopping to open the gate. A few yards from Sam she let go of her hold on her dresses to be able to throw her arms around her long, lost boy.

Samuel picked her off her feet and in swinging her around, again lost balance. Down they went together. Ruth, laughing and crying at the same time, all the while Henry standing on the porch with his mouth open.

It took some time before Henry fully understood what was happening. From his position on the porch, it looked like four people had lost their minds. He could tell that two of them were his parents. The other two he wasn't sure of, so he did what came naturally to him. He stood on the porch with his mouth open.

An hour after Samuel's arrival, everyone sat down to eat. Not wanting to track mud all over the house, they had decided to let the rain wash as much mud as possible off their clothes. It didn't take long with the heavy downpour.

There were so many things Josh's folks wanted to ask Samuel. One of the first, of course, was if he had heard anything of his brother James. Samuel took a swallow of milk, and then taking his mother's hand in his own said, "Ma, James and I were split the first week in the army.

"As you know, we took the train from Louisville to Gatling. From there we were lucky enough to get a job trailing some horses for the cavalry to Spartanburg. We wouldn't have taken the job, but since we were going in the same direction we figured the money wouldn't hurt.

"For two weeks we trailed those horses from sunup to sunset. I was comfortable with the saddle they gave me, but James got the raw end of the deal. You know how James is." Ruth nodded her head.

"I offered to trade with him, but he wouldn't hear of it. Said it was the luck of the draw. Anyway, when we got to Spartanburg, James' tailbone was so bruised and sore that he had a hard time sitting. When the recruiting sergeant asked James what he wanted to enlist as, James turned to me with that look he sometimes gets."

"I can just picture him," Ruth interrupted.

Samuel began again. "Well, James looked over at me and said, 'Sam, I've had enough sitting on a horse to last me the next ten years!' The recruiting sergeant overheard him.

"You can ride on a caisson," the sergeant had said at the time.

"Before James could say another word he was enlisted in the artillery. I told James I'd go with him, even though I don't like loud noises. But James insisted I take the cavalry, knowing how much I love horses. As it turned out I didn't have much choice. It was either that or be a ground pounder. There were no more spots open in the artillery. I gladly took the cavalry.

"James and I thought we would at least be together through training. No such luck. A couple days later he and his bunch were taken off one way, me and my bunch off another. I only saw James once after that.

"Was he all right?"

Yes, ma'am. It was right after a small skirmish that was almost the death of my boys and me. We had been caught watering our horses down in a gully. We hadn't seen hide nor hair of the enemy all day. Everything was nice and peaceful. Only sound was that of the horses drinking, when all of a sudden all heck broke loose!"

"What happened?" Henry asked excitedly.

"Johnny Reb had us surrounded except for an area that had a little thicket of scrub oak and briars. Guess they figured if they couldn't get through the briars, neither could we. Some of my boys tried to charge through the Rebs' lines, but were cut down before they got fifty yards. The only way we had to go was back toward the briars.

A sad look came over Samuel. "It looked pretty hopeless. The Rebs knew if they could get us all bunched up, they could take their time. It would be like shooting fish in a barrel.

"I got my men assembled as well as I could for one last charge. That way at least some might get through. I could hear the man next to me praying. Just as we were going to spur our animals on, a terrific explosion shook the ground, almost knocking us out of our saddles. I turned in time to see the next explosion go off about ten feet from the first.

"Right where the briar thicket had been, there was now clear ground with only a couple of shell holes. We turned our mounts and raced through the opening to our escape. It was an easy task for our horses to jump the shell craters.

"After we had regrouped, somebody made the remark that it was lucky for us that the Rebs had been as bad a shot with their artillery as they were. I said amen to that!"

"What did you do then?" It was Josh this time wanting to know.

"We took no time in circling around the ambush, and headed south to our rendezvous with our main unit. We hadn't gone more than a mile, when in the distance we saw dust rising. We took cover while I glassed the area. I'll never forget what I saw." Sam took another swallow of milk, while the rest of the family waited on the edge of their chairs.

"The dust was being thrown up from a four-horse team pulling a caisson and cannon. It was one of ours. We remounted and galloped up beside the cannon. When I looked over at the driver, I couldn't believe my eyes!

"Sitting on the box seat was none other than James, wearing the uniform of an artillery captain, although it was hard to tell with all the dust he was covered with. I wanted to stop right there, but since we had just gotten out of the fire, thought it best to get some ground between us and those Johnny Rebs. Besides, James was keeping his team at a good pace.

"A few minutes later we came within five hundred yards of being cut off by a company of Confederates. Lucky for us, there was no cavalry. James had known they were there and would come running when they heard his cannon go off. So he was getting out of there while he still could! It was several more miles before we dared let the horses rest.

"You should have seen his eyes light up when he saw me. After we hugged each other, I asked him how he happened to be out there all alone with just one scout."

"What did he say?" asked Pa.

"Here's what he told me: He had been back at his base camp when two scouts came in tellin' of the Rebs forming a skirmish line out by a creek five miles to the north. To the scouts it looked like the Rebs were setting a trap for someone. They tried to get the company commander to send a few platoons in behind them Rebs. He refused for some reason or other.

"Well, James heard what the scouts had to say, and thought a little artillery might be able to help out whoever the Rebs were lying for. James was the next ranking officer having got a battlefield commission. But try as he may, he couldn't get his superior to send help.

"So James decided to go it alone. When the commanding officer saw James heading out with a full team he tried to stop him, but by then James was going too fast for anyone on foot to catch him. A few miles later two of the scouts did catch up. Not to turn him back, mind you, but to help him set up when he got into location.

"When they got close to the ambush area, the fighting had already begun. James and the scouts galloped in as close as they dared behind the enemy. They set up with the team still harnessed. Seeing our predicament, they figured it better to get us out of there than to kill Johnny Reb. You know the rest of the story.

"We followed James back to his camp. I wasn't able to stay more than a few hours before I had to leave to find the rest of my company. That's all there is to tell. That's the last time I saw James in over a year."

Everyone looked down at the table, afraid to look each other in the eye. No one wanted to voice the fear they all felt at not knowing where James might be. It was an awkward time for the family. They wanted to rejoice at Samuel's return, yet were worried sick that James might not be coming home again.

It was Pa that was first to break the silence. "Let us all give thanks to our Lord that Samuel is home safe, and ask Him to bring James home, too." The family took each other's hands and bowed their heads in prayer.

Chapter VI

There was much to do around the homestead. With Sam home, things seemed to go much faster. There was a lightness in the air only daunted by the unknowing of James' whereabouts. He was a constant topic around the Templer home. When anyone spotted someone coming up the road or fence line, all work would stop until the stranger was identified as not being James.

Ruth was taking his absence the worst. When the men returned from their work, they would often see by the redness of her eyes that she had been crying. Then three weeks after Samuel's homecoming on a rainy, foggy day, nothing seemed to go right all morning.

Alice had found a hole in the fence and strayed from the pasture to the creek bottom where she got herself stuck in the mud. After finding her, it took several hours to drag her out. Pa and Sam tried everything but nothing seemed to work. In disgust, Pa roped her by the horns and pulled her out with the team. By this time, cold and hungry, the men cleaned up for the noon meal. An ominous feeling hung about the supper table and into the evening hours that night.

The next morning as the family was setting down for breakfast, they heard a knock at the door. All eyes turned toward the door, then back to each other sharing in that split second the same thought--James! Henry, who was closest to the door, was up like a rabbit spooked by dogs. On opening, the door revealed a small boy holding an envelope. Behind him a pony was tied to the porch railing.

"My pa said to fetch this up to you as fast as I could." Henry took it from the boy. John told Henry to bring the note to him. Inside was a telegram addressed to Mr. and Mrs. John Templer. It was from the Headquarters of the Army.

John turned to face his family, then realizing the boy was still standing in the doorway, motioned him in. "Come in and have a bite with us, boy."

"Thank you, sir. My pa did say they wanted an answer."

"Read it, John," his wife said, "we're waiting."

Pa turned the paper over in his hands. He was afraid of what it might say. He started to read. "It's from the Army!"

Ruth pulled her clasped hands up to her mouth. "Oh, dear, God! Is James all right?"

John shot a look in her direction. "I don't know, honey. I'll read the rest of it." He looked down at the telegram. "It says: 'Dear Mr. and Mrs. Templer. Sending telegram regards James Templer. Have names of men captured by Confederates. Captain James Templer's name on list. Dead.'" John's voice became quiet. "'Andersonville Prison Camp. Need you claim body. Sad regards. Capt. Elwood, U.S. Army. Wait answer.'"

No one spoke. What could they say? Here was news of the son they had been waiting for, hoping for his safe return. Now they knew. James was dead. John Templer bent over the table trying to hold back the tears. His oldest son was dead. How could it be? Why did it happen?

Sam took his mother in his arms and held her close. Josh and Henry stared at the top of the table. No words could say how each member of the Templer family felt. Their brother and son was gone. Never to return. Pa walked to the mantle where a small box of pencils were kept. Finding a sharp one, he carefully wrote an answer on the back of the paper.

"I told them we would come as soon as we could get things set here. You boys will have to take care of the place while Ma and I are gone." There was deep sadness in John Templer's voice. Samuel gave a look of agreement to his father. Josh and Henry both nodded their heads in answer.

It was two days before Ruth and John Templer could catch a train going west. Around the farm everyone was quiet and sullen. Samuel, being the oldest, would naturally take over Pa's place as head of the family while their parents were gone. It was a sad farewell as John and Ruth left to bring their eldest boy home.

James had always been full of joy and used humor to make any situation better. As the train pulled out from the station, John and Ruth sat back in their seats, each thinking their own thoughts. But most assuredly those thoughts were on the son they would never see laughing again. He would leave an empty spot in their hearts for the rest of their lives.

Ruth sat across from her husband in the rearward facing window seat clutching a bundle of James' clothes tied up in a small package. To passersby it might have looked as though the package contained her life savings. In fact, you could say in a way it did. John sat looking out the window, unseeing as the countryside sped by.

It would take two days by train, then another day and a half by coach to reach their final destination. Three and a half days of grief and sorrow. Then the many arrangements to be made for shipping the body back would take still another day.

The return journey would be the hardest knowing their son was in a sealed box in the baggage car. Ruth knew that John would want to ride in the back with his son, but she would need him with her to share her pain. The pain of a mother losing part of herself, her baby, now grown and died but her baby just the same.

Back home Josh and Sam kept themselves busy with chores around the farm. Neither of them dared talk of their brother, there was no need to. They felt the loss in their hearts, in their souls.

It was time for spring planting, and the boys got to it right after the folks departed for the train. Henry went with his parents as far as the train depot to bring the spring wagon back. He was just turning onto the north fork of the road which took him back home when he heard someone yell.

"Ho, boy! Hold up there a spell! I want to ask you something, boy!"

Henry turned to see Mr. Horstead coming up the lane on his old swayback mule named Joyce.

"Git up there, Joyce, Move along!"

Henry watched as old man Horstead urged the poor animal into a trot. The mule seemed the perfect mount for him, slow and unkempt. The animal from old age, Horstead by choice. Henry didn't know whether to stop and wait, or slap the team into a trot that was sure to leave the other man far behind. He decided to stop.

"What can I do for you, Mr. Horstead?"

"It's not you, but your brother Josh. That's who can do fer me, boy! He's got some explainin' to do.

I'll just ride along with you and have a talk with your folks." The last thing Henry wanted was the company of Mr. Horstead.

"My folks aren't home now, so no use coming round. They won't be back for near a week!"

"That so, boy?" Mr. Horstead was probing now. "Not fer a week ya say?"

"Yes, sir." Old man Horstead smiled a wry grin.

"In that case, I'll wait to see Josh till after your pa gets back. Well, get along, boy. Your brother will be worried if ya don't get home right away!"

Henry slapped the team into action, not looking back to see if Mr. Horstead was following. He was just glad to be away from the foul-smelling thief. Henry also realized that old man Horstead didn't know that Samuel was back from the war and he wasn't about to tell him.

Henry had an uneasy feeling deep in his gut about the meeting he just had with the head of the Horstead clan. I wonder what that old buzzard is up to, Henry wondered.

"Bring the team over here!" yelled Samuel as Henry approached the barn. Henry swung the Morgans around to where Sam had pointed. "Better water and feed them. We got a lot of work to do and we better get started as soon as possible. Still got ten acres to plant."

Henry unhooked the two Morgans from the springboard, letting the wagon tree drop to the ground with a thud.

"Pa ever see you treat the wagon like that and he'll be all over you. You know you can split the tree by dropping it the way you just did," Josh admonished Henry.

"Ah, Pa don't care if I drop it or not," Henry shouted. He was getting a little tired of his bigger brothers always telling him what to do.

Soon the two Morgans were hitched to the grain drill. Josh got busy filling the drill hoppers with fresh seed. After filling the drill, he checked to make sure the levers used to adjust the seed flow rate were working properly.

Pa, Sam, and Josh had taken turns the previous few days at the plow and harrow. Now the ground was set for the planting, with just enough moisture to insure that the seeds would sprout.

Samuel came over to where Josh was opening the last burlap sack of corn seed. "Everything okay?" he asked his younger brother.

"I'm ready when you are," Josh replied as he lifted the last of the seed into the hopper, letting a small amount spill over the edge and onto the ground. Samuel walked around the back of the planting machine, smoothing the seed with his hand until it was even all across.

One more check of the harness and Sam was satisfied that all was ready. Walking back to the head of the team he grabbed both sets of reins. He slid them through his hands until he came to the opposite ends, then holding them high he stepped into the loops, letting the weight of his body against them hold the horses back.

"All set, Josh?"

"All set. Let 'em go."

Josh stepped onto the rider's board attached to the rear of the drill. The Morgans walked lazily along not yet feeling the strain of the planter. Sam lined up the horses while Josh squeezed the disk handle lowering them to the ground. Behind him Henry swatted at the birds trying to feast on the newly sown kernels. For the moment all thoughts were lost in the work of the day.

The sun was setting as the boys finished the ten acres they had set to get done before evening. Weary from the strain of the day, they were eager to turn in for the night. Josh was the first to pull a bucket up from the well. Cupping his hands, he dug deep into the cool, fresh water the bucket contained. He was about to splash it on his face when he thought better. Instead he lifted the bucket over his head and let the water cascade down rinsing the dust and sweat from his hair.

"Feels good, doesn't it?" Sam had come up beside Josh.

"If you're done I think I'll do the same." Sam took the bucket from Josh and dropped it down the well.

"Come on over here, Hank." Sam motioned to Henry sitting on the front steps to the house.

"Might as well take your weekly bath while you're hot and dusty. Speakin' of dusty, you look like you just got out of Ma's flower bin."

Henry strolled over to where his older brother was holding the bucket, taking his shirt off as he walked.

"Why look at you, aren't you the little muscle man." Henry flexed his arm so his biceps enlarged, then laughed at himself.

"Am I ready to join the circus as their strong man, or should I wait a few more . . . " The blast of cold water cut him off in mid-sentence.

"That ought to shrink that big head of yours," Sam said laughing. It felt strange to be laughing and joking while their brother lay dead hundreds of miles away, but this was a hard land and sometimes you had to let your hair down just to get through the day.

The young men walked toward the house together, Sam between his two younger brothers with his arms outstretched around the two boys. It felt good to be home working the fields, the war an unreal memory from the past.

They were hungry, but too tired to cook anything or even make a fire, so they cut a loaf of bread into three large pieces. On this they heaped some cheese and a few slices of smoked ham, then covered the whole thing with some clover honey from the cupboard.

"Now all we need is some fresh milk and a good night's sleep," commented Josh. "Milk! Oh, no! I forgot to milk Alice this evening! She'll be standing out back of the barn waiting for me!" Josh took a bite of his sandwich and moved to get up.

"Stay there, Josh. I haven't milked a cow since me and James left home. I'll get her for you tonight." Josh sat back down in his chair.

"You don't have to, Sam. I can get her."

"No, you and Henry worked awful hard. Just take it easy. This one's on me."

Sam got up from the table. "I'm not that hungry right now anyway." He was remembering the day James and him left for the army and needed to be alone.

It was pitch dark, and Sam stumbled as he walked toward the back of the barn where he knew Alice would be waiting. As he got to the gate and fumbled with the latch, he could see her form at the feed stall.

"Hi, Alice, old girl. I'll get you inside and feed you some nice oats." He didn't mind talking to the cow, it made her relax and let her milk down. Sam stayed close to the fence, not wanting to step in anything fresh. The cow watched him come closely, anticipating the relief that was about to come.

In a few minutes Sam was sitting beside her pulling her teats in turn, splashing a stream of milk from each into the pail held between his legs. Every so often Alice would swat her tail in his direction, knocking his hat to the floor.

"Easy, girl, just about done, just a little more." Alice shifted her weight towards Sam almost upsetting the pail of milk.

"What's the matter, girl? Hear something outside?" Sam thought he heard a noise too from somewhere behind him. He reached over and pulled the lantern closer to his side.

Sam heard the noise again, this time for sure, like someone walking in the hay. The hair on the back of his neck stood on end. Now he felt, more than heard, the presence of someone or something behind him.

This feeling wasn't new to him. Once when he and his men were forced to take shelter for the night in an old earth works, he had felt this same feeling. He had turned just in time to see a Johnny Reb about to run him through with a bayonet.

He had dodged the thrusting spear by inches, seeing it bury itself to the hilt in the dirt beside him. He had instinctively reached for his sword, flinging the scabbard off and turning it to the other man's belly in one motion.

Sam had put all the strength he could behind the sword's thrust, not knowing how much force it would take to kill a man. As the sword dug deep into the man's stomach, Sam was sprayed with a gusher of blood that almost blinded him. He would never forget how the man's life blood smelled.

But here he was with no sword, only a pail of milk. He wanted to turn his head to see that which he was sure was behind him now. Ever so slowly he shifted his body around on the stool.

The blow took him by surprise. It moved Sam's body backward and away from Alice, who swished her tail where a second before his head had been. Sam tried to sit up but was unable to get his arms to work. He sunk back to the floor and into unconsciousness. A small pool of blood spread out from around his head. A hand reached down and turned out the lantern that had been upset by Sam's hand falling across it.

"Got to be more careful! You might start a fire and burn the place down. In fact, I think you will start a fire, but not till I get what I came after. Too bad you had to come out to milk the cow when you did, kid, but that's your problem now." The shadowy figure moved back to the corner where he had come from.

"I know your old man hides his cache in here somewhere. If it's here I'll find it, you can bet on that for sure, boy." The voice belonged to old man Horstead.

Josh and Henry finished eating and were about to go to bed when Henry asked why Sam wasn't back yet. Josh shrugged his shoulders as if to say, "I don't know."

“Maybe he couldn’t find Alice in the dark. She’s pretty used to me. Might have got spooked when Sam came out instead of me.” Josh was so tired, all he wanted to do was go to sleep, but now he resisted the urge.

“I better go help Sam find Alice or we’ll never get any rest!” With that he pulled his boots back on and went outside to find Sam.

He had just closed the door behind him when he saw the light from the lantern go out in the barn. Maybe Sam ran out of lamp oil. Josh lifted the lid of the large storage box that held the container of coal oil for the lamps. He pulled a small tin can out by its wire handle, being careful not to make any more noise than he had to. No use waking Henry up, he thought.

As Josh walked toward the barn, he noticed the barn door was standing wide open. That’s funny, he thought. I wonder why Sam left the door open. Doesn’t he know that the smallest wind will blow dust and dirt into the milk? Probably forgot, been so long since he did any milking around here.

Then Josh saw movement back to one side of the corral. Wasn’t one of our horses, they were in their stalls in the barn. He had seen to that himself. Josh put the tin can down beside him. Something didn't feel right and he better be prepared.

Edging down along the fence in a crouched position he moved closer to the silhouette. He could see it was an animal--a horse. No, a mule--old man, Horstead's mule for sure. But why would it be tied up here in the dark? Why hadn't Mr. Horstead hailed the house when he approached? Josh pulled a hand sickle out of the post where it had been stuck a few days before. Then slowly, ever so slowly he tiptoed to the open door.

Squatting just outside, he peered in to see if Sam was alone. Too dark. Josh would have to go in and light the lantern, but what of Horstead? What did all this mean?

Josh was just about to go in when he heard a rustling in the hay by the inside corner of the barn. He wanted to ask who's there, but thought better of it. Don't want to give myself away just yet, he thought.

Inside Sam was gaining consciousness. A moan escaped from his lips. Josh listened, another moan. This time Josh knew it was his brother and he was hurt.

He moved into the barn, still holding the sickle in his left hand, while his right hand searched in his pocket for a match. Finding one, he struck it to the side of the sickle blade, lighting up the barn with its light.

"Josh?! Then who's that on the floor?" The voice from behind startled Josh. He hadn't seen Sam on the floor yet. Josh turned to confront Mr. Horstead.

"What are you doing here? You got no business being here this time of night or any other time when Pa's not here! What have you done to Sam?"

"So it was Samuel milkin' the cow. Didn't figure him to be home. Don't make no never mind to me though, one body or two, makes no difference!"

Josh glanced around looking for Sam, finally finding him laying over by Alice. The match was starting to burn his fingers. Josh shook the match out and quickly took another from his pocket, lighting it the same way as before. He held it over his head so he could see Horstead better. Josh knew full well the thief was planning to do away with him and Sam.

Horstead reached behind his back and in slow motion brought out the throwing knife he always kept there. Josh knew he had to do something to stop

Horstead before it was too late. As the man brought the weapon up to throwing position, Josh pivoted on his feet bringing the sickle up and around with all the force he could muster before releasing it, hoping to cause Horstead to dodge it and thereby miss his target. In spinning around, the match in Josh's hand went out, leaving the barn in total darkness.

Got to get out of here and to the house where the guns are kept, he thought. Josh darted at full speed toward the house, yelling to Henry to get out of bed. In through the door Josh flew almost knocking Henry over in the press.

"Bolt the door!" he yelled. "Old man Horstead's out there trying to kill us!" Henry threw his body into the door slamming it shut with a bang.

"Quick, bolt it!" Josh didn't know how close Horstead was following behind him. It took Josh only a minute to charge his squirrel rifle, but it seemed like an hour. Both boys got set for Horstead's attack. Five minutes went by, but still no footsteps on the porch. Finally as Josh was about to peak out to see what was happening, he was stopped by a sound out on the porch.

"Git ready!" he told his little brother. "If he tries to break down the door, I'll send a round right through it! You better get Pa's .50 ready just in case!"

Henry slipped to the back of the room and quickly got the .50 from on top of the mantle where it was kept along with a couple of loading boards holding five greased mini balls each.

Josh threw his powder horn to Henry so he wouldn't have to expose himself to the window on that side of the room. Josh in his haste had forgotten about the window.

"Turn the lamp down low and get in the shadows!" he ordered his younger brother.

"Where's Sam?" Henry asked.

"Out in the barn! He's hurt real bad, might even be dead by now," Josh told him. Henry started to cry.

"Don't do that," Josh whispered. "I need you to help me. You can cry later if we get through this alive."

Again came the sound of footsteps on the porch coming closer to the door. Josh squatted down while lining the rifle up on the door.

"Here, this one's ready," Henry said pushing the .50 along the floor to where Josh was. Josh didn't have to ask if Henry had loaded the rifle correctly. Out in the country that's one of the first things a child is taught, a tradition from the time when one still had to fear attacks from Indians.

Now the man was just outside the door. The boys got ready. Josh had traded his .32 caliber for the .50 his brother passed to him. He reached up and carefully pulled the hammer on the Hawkins' back. He could feel the triggers one by one cock into place.

Shouldering the butt tight against him, he pulled the rear-most trigger until he heard it click, making the front one a hair trigger. Inching his finger through the trigger guard, he lined the sights up on the middle of the door while being careful not to let his finger touch the hair trigger.

"Come a few steps closer and I'll blow your guts all over the place," Josh said to himself under his breath. He placed his finger on the trigger ever so softly, expecting it to go off any second.

"Help! Josh! Henry! Help me!" It was Sam's voice, then there was a falling sound and all was quiet. Henry looked at Josh.

"Is old man Horstead trying to trick us?" Josh asked as he took his finger off the trigger and placed it vertically over his mouth.

They listened. All was still. Josh motioned for Henry to open the door while staying out of the line of fire. When the door was opened only a crack Josh could see it was Sam lying on the porch. Still, Horstead might be hiding just out of sight! But he couldn't let Sam just lay out there!

"Turn out the lamp!" he told Henry. Now all was dark. Josh would have to chance it.

"Open the door and when I pull Sam in, close it and bolt it quick!" In a few seconds Sam lay inside and the door was again securely fastened.

"See to Sam," Josh told Henry. "I'll get some help over here pronto. Where's Pa's six-shooter?"

"In the drawer by the bed."

Josh felt his way to the table. Opening the drawer, he withdrew the .36 caliber Remington. Good, it's loaded already. I'm going to fire three shots from the attic window. Anybody hear them, they'll come running with some of the other neighbors."

Josh pulled the table over so he could get height enough to gain access to the attic. Soon he was able to pry the window open, being careful not to expose himself as a target.

Aiming the handgun high, he fired three consecutive shots. Gunshots would travel for miles this late at night when all else was quiet. Then he waited. Within minutes he heard the sound of horses moving across the fields, coming fast.

"Ho, the house!" a voice called. "What's the trouble?"

"That you, Mr. Riehl? asked Josh.

"It's me, boy. Benjamin. I got Art Johnson, Roy Talley, and his two boys with me. What's going on?"

Josh told them he would meet them on the porch, feeling sure that old man Horstead would be on his way home after seeing the riders come up. After Josh told Ben the story of what happened and after they had seen to Samuel, Benjamin Riehl and the rest of the men followed Josh to the barn. Roy carried a lamp to light the way.

As they approached the barn they saw Joyce the mule still tied to the fence.

"Where did you see that Horstead rascal?" Benjamin asked.

Josh pointed toward where Horstead had been standing when he tried to throw the knife. There against the wall was old man Horstead, his legs limp and his body held in place by the sickle imbedded in the wall. A river of blood had flowed from his Carotid Artery down his side and into the hay. A trickle of blood followed the sickle blade around his neck. The old thief's eyes were open.

Chapter VII

Ruth Templer was choking on the dust. It had been unusually dry in this part of the country. At the last relay station there was water only for the horses. Now the dust and thirst made the Templers' journey even more miserable.

"You folks all right down there?" The stage driver leaned far out on his seat and looked down at the four passengers covered in grime. He asked again thinking his fare hadn't heard him. "You all right down there?"

John Templer leaned out the window. "We could use some water for the women folk. They can't take much more of this dust and heat."

The driver pulled himself upright, not bothering to acknowledge John. "Whoa, you mule heads," he commanded the horses. The stage soon slowed to a stop and the driver jumped down. Walking to the rear of the stage, he soon produced a small cask marked Colonel William P. Pelky, Army Depot, Gainsborough, N.C.

"This oughta fix us all up a little. I was getting dry myself." The cask had a leather thong tied to a wooden spout. Using the handle of his Colt, the driver soon had the spout pounded into the cask.

"I ain't got but one cup. But I'll rinse it good, then the ladies can use it first." He smiled a kind smile at Ruth and the other lady. "Mind you, no one's to know about this. It would be my job! If word was to get back to anyone, especially old Pelky, I'd be fired on the spot! But I can't let the ladies suffer for some high an' mighty colonel that won't drink none of the water around him. Says it's poisoned, thinks the war's still on." The driver shook his head at the thought.

"Course, when it was, you couldn't of dragged him down here with two teams of horses! Only come down to play big shot after it was nice and safe. You know the kind, no guts, all glory. Just like most politicians." He finished rinsing the cup, filled it, and handed it to Mrs. Templer.

"Thank you." Mrs. Templer raised the cup to her lips. It wasn't cool but it helped to revive her spirits a little.

"Take your time, ma'am. The horses can use a little breather in this heat anyway." The driver took a piece of cloth from his back pocket and poured a little water on it. He handed it to Ruth.

"For your face," he said. He did the same for the other woman. While the women were cleaning up, he motioned the men to the rear of the coach.

"I thought you gents might like somethin' a might stronger." He produced a small, flat container from his other back pocket. Handing the flask to John, he motioned for him to take a swig. John took a shallow sip, then passed it to the other man.

"Won't cool you off, but it'll make things a bit easier on you gents," the driver said with a smile. The other man took a long pull on the container.

"Mighty good stuff, but aren't you afraid you're really putting your job in jeopardy by giving your passengers whiskey?" It was the other man speaking.

"Jeopardy? What do you mean, 'jeopardy'?"

"Get yourself fired, lose your job!"

"Well, if that's what you mean, why didn't you just come right out and say it then No, I ain't worried about getting canned for this." He held up the flask.

"This here's company stock. They give it to us to give the passengers a snort now and then, 'specially if they have to get out and push the stage over some bad ground. It's the water they better not get wind of!" The driver gave the man a hard look. "I'd be through for sure if they did!" The driver offered the men another drink. John raised his hand in refusal, the other man took the flask to his lips. With two swallows it was dry.

"Ya don't say!" the driver shook his head in disgust, throwing the flask to the side of the trail.

"Better get on board, we got some time to make up." He stopped by the side of the coach. "Not a word about the water, mind you!"

John opened the door so the other man could get in, then stepped up himself. "Let her rip!" he yelled to the driver, and they were on their way again.

"Feeling better, dear?" John took his wife's hand in his. Ruth looked at her husband's hands, then his face. She had loved that face for as long as she could remember from the very first time she had seen him some 25 years before. It was a face any woman would be proud of, strong, yet gentle. It made her feel very secure, and now in this time of great need, she would have to hold on to that security very tightly.

"Twenty miles to go, folks! We'll make one more stop to rest and water the horses."

The four people glanced at each other as if to say, "I'm glad it's almost over."

The stagecoach had been following a road alongside a dried up creek bottom to its left. Now as John pulled the curtain back, he could see that the creek took a hard turn to the right and crossed through the stage's right of way. He could see no bridge ahead. The stage was already slowing to a halt.

"Everybody out! The horses will need our help getting across the creek bottom. You women can wait for us on the other side, the men will have to push." The driver had dismounted and was standing beside the lead horses. "I'll ease them into it. When the back wheels hit bottom, shove like mad."

John helped the two ladies out of the coach. The man was sound asleep. "Mister! Gotta get out and help." The man opened his eyes, then shut them again.

"I ain't helping shove no coach anywhere," the man said through half-parted lips. John clenched his teeth. The muscles in his jaw stood out.

"Mister, I don't feel like arguing about it. Get out of there now!" The man could see John meant business.

"All right! I'll get out, but I ain't pushing. We paid for a ride, not a walk." He got out and walked over to the shade of a tree where he sat down. The driver looked at John. He could see John was a man of action, and the fur was about to fly. John seemed to gather strength, then walked directly to where the man sat. In one quick motion, he grabbed the back of the man's shirt and hoisted him off the ground.

"You'll darn well push!" John dragged the man through the dirt to the back of the coach and let him drop. "The body of my son is just up ahead, and I aim to see him as soon as I can!" The man picked himself up from the dirt, his eyes showed he had too much to drink.

"If he's dead, then what's the rush? He'll keep." The man realized he had said the wrong thing, but it was too late to change things now. John Templer looked into the man's watery eyes.

"If you weren't a sniveling drunk, I'd bash your face in. Now get behind that wheel and push!" The drunkard leaned into the wheel. "Slap those horses!" John yelled. The stage lunged forward then settled into a rut. They tried again, this time the wheels came half out of the rut before settling back in. The driver came back to have a look. He rubbed his three-day old growth of beard while pondering what to do next.

"Looks like we'll have to unload her. Too heavy this way." He started to unfasten the canvas back.

"Let me push, maybe with the extra help we can get it out." John looked over at his wife lifting her skirts as she gingerly stepped down into the creek bottom. "Where do you want me to push?" she asked her husband. John pointed to a place just behind the front wheel.

"Be careful. If it starts to come back on you, get out of the way fast."

Ruth looked at him and smiled. "All right, dear," she said. With the combined force, the coach moved slowly out of the rut and onto the middle of the creek bed.

"Everyone get back!" the driver hollered. "I'll have to get a runnin' start at the other bank. Be ready to help the horses if it looks like we're not going to make it up the other side." He climbed back up on his high perch of a seat. "Git up you muleheads!" he screamed at the top of his lungs. The horses darted forward as he slapped the reins down hard on their rumps. Up the other side the team scrambled, pulling the coach along with them.

Just as the stage was about to top the embankment, the left rear wheel caught on a rock, bringing the coach to an abrupt stop. The three people quickly took their positions and pushed as hard as they humanly could. The coach slipped back, but still they pushed. It seemed to be of no use. The coach was slowly but steadily moving backward into the creek bed.

"My dress!" yelled Mrs. Templer. "It's caught under the wheel!"

As the coach moved rearward, it was rolling over Ruth's long travel dress, pulling her under the wheel. John shifted his hold so he could see what was happening to his wife. The stage was obviously going to crush her if it moved much more.

"Oh, dear God! Give me strength," John muttered, as he braced himself. Taking a deep breath, he lifted up on the stage with all his strength. "It's too heavy!" yelled the man next to him, who now had his back to the coach and was pushing with all his might. We can't stop it!"

The veins in John's neck stood out as though they would burst, his forehead was beaded with sweat. Still he lifted. He could feel the steel brace cut deep into his hands as the rear of the stage started moving ever so slowly off the ground. For what seemed like hours he pulled up on the tremendous weight. The stage rose higher and higher over the rock. With the rear wheels free from their trap, the coach was able to move a few feet forward.

Ruth pulled herself free and jumped to safety. As soon as John Templer saw that his wife was safe he lowered the stage to the ground, Ruth ran to his side, there were tears in her eyes.

"It's all right, honey. You're safe now." John lifted his hand to wipe a tear form his wife's cheek. Their eyes met.

"I love you," Ruth whispered to John. Then she saw the deep cuts in John's hands. "Dear, God!" she exclaimed. "Let me help you." Ruth tore a piece of her underskirt off and bandaged her husband's hands.

It took another hour before the driver working with a shovel was able to set the coach totally free. Once everything was reloaded on the stage, the driver went back and got the cask of water.

"Might as well drink our fill, can't take this here barrel any further. I'll have to tell the station master that old Pelky's water fell off when we were crossing the creek and sprung a leak. Nothing I could do about it, either drink what was left or let it go to waste. Any objections?" he was looking at the second man.

"None from me," the drunk said. "After seeing what this man did when he lifted the stage, I figure even if I had to walk the rest of the way, it would be worth it. I'll remember him lifting the stage off the ground as long as I live." The man turned toward John. "Mister, I'm mighty sorry for letting my rear end overload my mouth like I did. I hope you and your Misses will accept my apology. I guess that whiskey got the best of me." He held out his hand. John took it and both men shook.

"We're in troubled times, your apology accepted. Now let's get on board or you might have to walk after all."

Once underway, the ladies became interested in some needlepoint while John and the other man, who had produced a deck of cards decided to play a friendly game of poker, but had to give it up after a few minutes as the deck only had one ace in it. Templer wondered about that.

"What did you say your name was? the man asked John.

"John Templer, and this is my wife, Ruth."

"Glad to meet you, John, Ruth." He tipped his hat in the direction of Ruth.

"My name's John Sherman, Dr. John Sherman. Dentist by trade, gambler by choice."

"What brings you way out here?" John Templer asked.

"Heading down to the dry country. Consumption's got a grip on me, the dry air is supposed to help."

John had noticed the man's sporadic coughing.

"Mighty hot for this time of the year. You suppose it's like this all the year round?" Sherman wiped his forehead with a small white handkerchief he produced from his pocket. He folded the kerchief and placed it back in his pocket, then waited for John to answer his question. John never responded to Sherman's question. He seemed lost in thoughts of some other place, some other time.

"John, did you hear me?" John looked toward the other man.

"You talking to me?"

Sherman could see that John Templer was still not fully aware that he had been spoken to. "I was just wondering about the weather. Is it always this hot down here or is this a fluke of nature?"

John looked outside as if somehow to find the answer out there. His mind just wasn't working at this moment, he had other things, more important things, on his mind.

"I don't rightly know, doctor. Never been through here before."

Sherman could see it wasn't much use trying to start up a conversation. "Go back to sleep, John."

"Huh?"

"Nothing, John. Didn't say a thing."

Ruth looked over at her husband and smiled. She too was feeling the terrible pain inside, knowing that they would soon be with their oldest son, James. Up until now she could tell herself that James really wasn't dead. There had been a terrible mistake. It was someone else in the pine box stored in the ice cellar at the end of the stage line. She wanted to cry, to let it all come flooding out, but knew she had to be strong.

"Whoa, you darn muleheads! Whoa now." The team slowed to a trot. "Gotta cool these varmints down before we get to the depot!" the driver yelled back. "Remember, not a word about the water."

Off in the distance John Templer could see several small buildings. There was much activity around them. Smoke was coming from one of the smaller buildings, the cook house, John figured.

"Must be the army depot just ahead, about three quarters of a mile," John told his wife. Fear showed in her eyes, and in one corner he could see a tear just starting its run down her cheek. She caught it before it rolled very far.

The horses were at a walk now. John Templer's gut was tied in knots. "God give me strength," he prayed under his breath.

The stage pulled up at the front door of the army depot. A slender man stepped off the broad, wooden porch and opened the door of the coach. He was wearing the stripes of an army supply sergeant. He held a small book in his hand and glanced down reading something from it.

"Any of you the Templers?" he asked.

"We're the Templers, sergeant," John answered as he stepped out of the coach and turned to take his wife's hand.

"Please follow me, sir." The sergeant waited until Ruth was out of the coach, then motioned them toward the open door. The room was barren except for a large desk with a padded leather chair behind it. Smaller chairs were scattered around. On each side of the room across from one another were two small windows. John Templer noticed that someone sitting behind the desk would be able to see anyone approaching from either direction on the road. Once inside he asked them to be seated, then poured them some coffee. "I'll get you some grub, you must be starved."

"We want to see our son." It was Ruth speaking.

"Honey, you better eat some food. You haven't eaten enough to keep a bird alive."

"John, I want to see James!" She started to cry. The sergeant standing close by broke in.

"Ma'am, that won't be possible for several hours. Please have something to eat, it will help you feel better."

"Why can't we see our boy?" Ruth's tear-soaked eyes fixed on the sergeant.

"It's the colonel, ma'am. He gave orders not to open the icehouse until he's here. Sorry, folks, nothing I can do till he gets back. Please don't be mad at me. If I could, I would. I hope you believe me, it's the truth, swear to God."

John walked over to his wife and placed his hand on her shoulder. "It's all right, honey. Eat something. We can wait." She placed her hand over his.

"All right, John, I'll eat. But I want to see our boy as soon as that man gets here."

"We'll take the food now," John told the soldier. The sergeant left the room and returned shortly with two plates of fried chicken and some corn on the cob.

"The cook will be bringing a pitcher of milk. Hope the food's to your liking." He then excused himself, turned, and left the building.

John was tired of sitting so he took his plate and walked over to the west window. As far as the eye could see, there was nothing but flat treeless land, only the road dissected the sameness. Standing there, looking at the road as it ran off into the distance, John seemed to be mesmerized.

"Someone's coming." John could see a small black dot on the road followed by a cloud of dust. "Maybe it's the colonel." He walked over and set the plate down on an empty chair. "You wait in here, Ruth.

I'll wait outside to see if it's him." John walked out leaving his wife to finish her food.

The black dot soon took on the appearance of a large touring buggy, top down and complete with a matched team of four draft horses. An escort of six soldiers followed in a neat column of two's. Four behind and two ahead. One of the soldiers in the front carried a staff with the Union flag flying from it. John Templer watched as the whole affair came closer. A very impressive sight, thought John.

The buggy pulled up opposite to where John stood. The driver sat erect, unmoving, as though made of wood like the Indian in front of some tobacco stores. Behind him in the rear of the buggy sat a distinguished looking gentleman, although rather large around the middle, in every way still looking like one would expect a colonel to look. Almost before the buggy came to a halt, the sergeant was at its side.

"Welcome back, sir. The Templers are waiting inside. They're anxious to see the remains of their son. They're not too happy about having to wait for your return, sir. And frankly, I don't blame them, sir."

"Son, if I want your opinion, I'll ask for it. Until then be advised to keep it to yourself. I didn't make colonel by not knowing the right thing to do. Has the photographer gotten here yet, sergeant?"

"Yes, sir. He's in the bunkhouse getting his equipment together. May I ask what he's here for, sir?"

"This man's Army doesn't pay you to ask questions. And it doesn't pay me to answer your questions either. Now go tell him we'll be ready in about ten minutes."

Yes, sir!" The sergeant saluted the officer, then turned on his heels and left to give the message to the photographer. "Big blowhard jackass!" he said aloud as soon as he turned the corner of the building.

John Templer went back in the building and waited by his wife. In a few minutes the colonel, followed by his adjutant, strutted into the room.

"Mr. and Mrs. Templer, I'm Colonel Pelky. First, may I offer my heart-felt condolence on the death of your son . . ." He looked to his aide.

"James, sir."

"Ah, yes, Sergeant James."

"Captain James Templer, Artillery Division, sir," the aide cut in.

"Yes, as I was saying, I'm sorry about your boy." The colonel was visibly flustered, he took out a handkerchief and wiped his brow. John noticed he kept glancing out the door as if he was expecting someone.

"Yes, I believe we're ready now. Won't you please follow my aide? He'll show you where you can see your son."

John and Ruth followed the adjutant outside to where a small party of troopers stood at attention, sabers in hand. John didn't see the photographer setting his camera up a short distance away. The adjutant, Lieutenant Carver, asked them to stand in front of the line of soldiers.

"We'll bring your son's coffin out here, Mr. Templer." Ruth grabbed her husband's arm.

"Not out here, John. Don't let them bring James out here in front of everyone." John looked down at his wife.

"I won't let them, dear. Lieutenant Carver, I need to speak to you." Carver walked over to John and Ruth.

"May I help you, sir?"

"Yes, we want to see our son in privacy." Carver looked at John for a moment without speaking. The look of surprise showed on his face.

"The colonel won't like that, Mr. Templer. He has a ceremony planned. It cost the Army a lot of money. No, he won't like that at all." John looked the man right in the eye.

"It cost us our oldest son. Now, I don't care what the colonel has planned. We will see our boy in private."

"Just a minute, sir, I'll be right back." The junior officer turned his back on John and walked briskly away toward the colonel's office.

John heard one of the soldiers say, "He walks like a Banty Rooster, doesn't he?" Some of the other troopers laughed at the remark.

Shortly the officer emerged from the building and advanced to face John Templer. "Sir, the colonel said that you may have all the time you need with your son after the ceremony."

John took a deep breath, then started at a fast walk toward the building the adjutant had just come from. The officer, taken off guard, now tried to catch up and with John. He trotted past John, turned around and walked backwards trying to reason with him. John pushed him to the side, only to be confronted with him again. Just before they reached the steps, the officer again tried to reason while in his backward gait. His heel slammed into the lower step and caused him to sprawl out over the porch. This, of course, brought a roar from the men lined up in front.

"I'll . . ." the executive started, shaking his fist at John.

"You'll do what?!"

The man could see John was in no mood to be fooled with. Besides, John outweighed the man by sixty pounds of rock-hard muscle while the officer was flabby from years of attending the many fashionable social events in Washington, D.C. He knew he was outmatched in every way.

"Sir, I am an officer and a gentleman. I will not roughhouse with you. It's beneath me."

John stared down at the man sprawled on the porch. "You're nothing but a fat pig in a man's suit.

You're a disgrace to the uniform, and if you don't get out of my way, I'll kick your butt."

The man scurried out of the way. In two steps John was at the door. Before he could enter, the adjutant ordered the men to surround John. They came on the run. John Templer was prepared to fight them all if that was what it took to see his boy.

"Hold up there men. I'd think twice before I did anything rash." The men, along with John, turned to see who it was that was doing the talking. The colonel joined the adjutant who was now standing just outside the circle of men surrounding John. There standing a dozen feet away stood Dr. Sherman.

"You can't order my men around, mister! Maybe you want to join your friend here in the guard house." Sherman smiled a big smile flashing pearl-white teeth that were uncommon in those days.

"Maybe so, but sooner or later my uncle is bound to hear about it and that wouldn't be too good for you, Colonel." The Colonel's face started to flush.

"Just what can this uncle of yours do about anything?"

Sherman stood there grinning. "You might say he has a lot of pull in Washington." The colonel threw his chest out like a turkey running a bluff.

"I know everybody in Washington and I don't think any uncle of yours could be worth spit. Now what did you say your name was?"

Dr. Sherman kept smiling. "My name was, and still is, Sherman--Dr. John Sherman. And my uncle's name was, and still is, Sherman--first name William, like in General William T. Sherman. You might know him as Bill Sherman. You do know him, don't you?" The colonel's mouth dropped open.

"I'll be writing him in a few days. Would you want me to mention you, Colonel? I'm sure he would be very interested in how you're doing down here. He's very interested in the South you know, especially how the Army is doing. Seems to have an interest in the Army, kind of like it was his own or something.

"That won't be necessary, Dr. Sherman. I'll be sending him a complete report in a few days. I'm sure he'd rather hear about your trip."

"That's very kind of you. Now what was it you wanted with my friend here?" he nodded towards John.

"Just a misunderstanding by the lieutenant. I was on my way out to escort them personally to their son when this unfortunate mistake took place. Now Mr. and Mrs. Templer, if you will please follow me, I'll see to it that you're not disturbed."

The colonel marched across the yard to the icehouse. John followed after him taking Ruth's hand in his as they walked. The colonel took a large brass key from his pocket and unlocked the padlock on the door, then swung the door open so the Templers could enter.

"I'll take the lock, colonel. Wouldn't want to get locked in by accident." The senior officer handed him the lock.

"By all means, I'll send a man down to break the lead seals on the coffin. We have to seal them that way to keep--" the Colonel realized what he was about to say and stopped short. "Well, you know what I mean."

He came to attention, saluted John and Ruth, then turned briskly on his heel and walked away. The icehouse was dark and foreboding. Like most icehouses in the warmer climates, the building was only to conceal a large pit beneath it. By placing the ice below ground, the ground became a natural insulator allowing the ice to stay frozen much longer. From the doorway, a ladder descended into the darkness. A soldier came over and handed John a lantern, it was already lit.

"I'll go down first and take the seals off, sir."

"Don't you want the lantern, soldier?" John started to hand the lamp back to the private now starting down the ladder.

"No, sir! I get nervous enough just knowing all them bodies are down there. I sure don't want to see them, too. I know where your son's box is, it was all set to come out for the ceremony when you got here."

Ceremony, John wondered. In quick order the man was out of sight in the darkness. The Templers could hear the sounds of prying. Before long, the trooper was again at the top of the ladder. "Be careful, ma'am, it's a long drop to the bottom." John looked at his wife.

"I understand if you would like to wait up here, Ruth," John told his wife.

"That's my firstborn down there. I want to go to him now, I'm not afraid of the darkness." Her husband led helping his wife down the ladder. At the bottom with the light held high over his head, John could see several dozen pine boxes stacked one on another. Large blocks of ice were scattered between the coffins. High overhead he could see a block and tackle fashioned to a stout beam used to lower the ice into the hole. It was also used to lower the bodies down for storage, and when the time came to hoist them out again.

To one side a coffin lay by itself. The name crudely painted on the side read: "J. Templer, Captain, U.S. Army." The seals were broken and the lid was pried partially up. Ruth let out an involuntary gasp when she saw the coffin. John reassured her, then bent down over the burial box.

"Ruth, you don't have to look."

"Open the lid, John. I want to see my boy." The cover came loose easily in John's strong hands. He took the lamp and lifted it over the inert form, the body was covered with a blue Army blanket. John reached out to his wife and pulled her close. Ruth looked at her husband, "Go ahead," she said. John carefully pulled the blanket down so they could see the face beneath it. The face looking back from the coffin--was that of a black man.

John stood up and turned toward the doorway high above. Cupping his hands around his mouth he yelled, "Ho up there!" Soon a silhouette of a man appeared outlined in the doorway.

"Do you need some help down there?" It was the sergeant's voice.

"Better bring the colonel, there's been a big mistake." The sergeant started down the ladder.

"Let me see what you're talking about. The colonel's so afraid of your friend that he's hiding out in the cook shed, hoping Sherman will get the stage out of here in an hour. Boy, Sherman's really got him spooked."

The sergeant was quickly beside the coffin next to where Ruth was standing. He asked John for the light, then swung it over the corpse. "Oh, Lord! I see what you mean. What I don't see, is how it could have happened." The sergeant excused himself and went back up the ladder and out of sight.

"John, do you know what this means? James may still be alive. I've had a feeling in my heart that he isn't dead. Now I'm sure of it."

"I hope you're right, honey, but maybe we shouldn't get our hopes up too high until we're sure." John looked into his wife's eyes. For the first time since they received the telegram, her eyes looked alive. "Let's get out of here and get some fresh air. I'm starting to shiver." Funny he hadn't felt the cold before.

Emerging from the darkness to the bright light outside seemed as though they were coming back from Hell itself. Only the devil wasn't down there. He was a short distance from the icehouse door in the uniform of a Union colonel, presently in an animated conversation with the sergeant. After a brief argument with the sergeant, he came over to where the Templers were standing.

"My sergeant tells me the body down there is not your son James. That's impossible. The Army doesn't make mistakes like that. My report of his death says that he was killed when a cannon was hit by an exploding shell fired from the Rebs' lines. What I'm trying to say, Mr. and Mrs. Templer, is that your boy is bound to look different. It's a wonder his whole head wasn't blown off, pardon the expression, ma'am."

"Have you seen the body, colonel?" John watched as the colonel shifted his weight from one foot to the other.

"No, Mr. Templer, I haven't seen how he looks, but I'm sure it's your son. The coffin does have his name on it, doesn't it?"

John Templer was getting disgusted with the whole affair. He didn't give a damn who it was or wasn't in the coffin, he knew it wasn't his son. What he did give a damn about, however, was if his son wasn't here, where the heck was he? Was he dead or alive, sick or wounded?

"Yes, it certainly has my son's name on it or at least the same name as my son, but I'm telling you it's not my son in that box. Now a man should know his own flesh and blood . . ."

"And a mother would know her son no matter how badly he might look. A mother would know for sure!" Ruth broke in.

"Maybe you ought to go down there, colonel, and have a look for yourself." The colonel glanced over to where John Sherman leaned against the corner of the icehouse smoking a long black cigar, his wide-brimmed hat pulled down over his eyes so that his face was partially hidden. It gave him the look of something sinister, something the colonel didn't want to anger.

"I think I will go down and have a look for myself. Maybe I can clear this matter up, might just be that the wrong coffin was opened in the dark." The officer hoped that this maneuver would satisfy Dr. Sherman. The last thing in the world he wanted was to have news of this get back to the President.

As he approached the open doorway, he could hear the shouting of the stage driver urging his team down the road. Just great, he thought. Now I'm stuck with that bastard Sherman for another day. He stuck his head into the darkness trying to see the bottom where the coffins were. Without the lamp he was unable to see more than half the ladder's length where it descended into the cavity.

"Corporal, bring a couple of men and hoist the coffin up here where the light's better. We'll get to the bottom of his once and for all."

In a matter of minutes, the coffin was lifted out of its dungeon and into the bright sunlight. The colonel squatted by the coffin and examined the edge of the lid. "I thought you told me you looked at the body. I don't see how that can be with the lid still nailed shut." The sergeant stepped forward and came to attention alongside his colonel.

"Sir! If it pleases the colonel, sir, we had to nail the top back on to keep the body from falling out when we pulled it up, sir! I'll have a man unseal it immediately, sir."

John Templer thought it funny that the sergeant showed such respect for his superior, when earlier it had been more than evident that the sergeant despised this glory seeking, gutless wonder. John suspected there was more to this than met the eye. He figured to just keep quiet and let the scene play out.

He was also curious as to why John Sherman was paying so much attention to the photographer's camera and flash tray. The photographer appeared to be showing him how to load the flash tray with the fine grain black powder used to make the brilliant flash that stopped action, even with the primitive cameras of the day. Every once in a while, Sherman and the photographer would laugh at a private joke they shared between them.

"The lid's loose, sir." It was one of the troopers speaking. "Shall I open it up?" The commanding officer bent over and grabbed the edge of the coffin lid.

"I'll do it myself, soldier. Then he addressed himself to Ruth Templer. "Ma'am, maybe you should wait in my office. Now that it's up here in the light, it won't be a pretty sight."

"Don't worry about me, colonel. That's not my boy in there. I'm sure he's alive somewhere." The officer pursed his lips in defiance.

"Ma'am, I hate to sadden you more than you already are, but your son is in this pine box. That's the simple fact of the matter. If you want to stay and watch, I guess that's your prerogative." By now Dr. Sherman had moved along with the photographer to a spot about ten feet from the group gathered by the box. The colonel was unaware of their presence.

John Templer was starting to get the picture, he said nothing. The officer took off the lid, then slowly pulled down the blanket without looking at the corpse. At the very same moment, there was a blinding flash followed by a cloud of smoke.

"What was that?" Colonel Pelky asked. Then he caught sight of the photographer pulling the glass negative out of his camera. Sherman was still holding the flash tray, he had a big smile on his face.

"What did you take a picture of?" the colonel asked wiping his eyes, still partially blinded from the flash. The flash from the exploding power had blinded him before he saw the corpse, so he was still unaware of what the coffin held.

"Just wanted to get a picture for my story, colonel. Didn't mean to bother you."

The colonel remembered the talk he and the picture taker had had before the Templers arrived. They had discussed the story that was to appear in several newspapers around Washington, D.C. It was to read something like this:

The People's Colonel

Colonel E. Pelky has taken on the sad task of returning the bodies of our soldiers lost in combat to their heart-grieved families. Says Colonel Pelky, "As these men's leader, I feel that I should be the one to help ease the burden from the families of these American heroes whose lives were given in defense of our great land." An admirable gesture from a great American leader.

The story was to go on giving facts and figures about this great colonel. Of course, it would not reveal the fact that while most soldiers were in the fields fighting battles, and many of them dying, Colonel E. Pelky was fighting his battles in the ballrooms and bedrooms of the Capital. He did have many a close call though, mostly when someone's husband came home too soon.

"Did you get a good one, or do you want to try another angle?" the colonel asked, still not seeing the body under the blanket.

"I think this is all I'll need. Thank you, sir, for your cooperation. I'm sure the folks back home will like this picture very much." And with that he pulled the legs of his tripod together and carried the whole affair towards his waiting buckboard.

The colonel watched him go, thinking it strange that he didn't want another picture. After all, the officer felt he was important news to the people back at the Capital. As the enlisted men were fond of saying, "He was a legend in his own mind."

John and Ruth Templer waited for the colonel to get back to the business at hand, especially the reaction that was sure to come when the colonel finally took a look at what was in the box at his side.

When is he going to look, for heaven's sake, thought John. The colonel sensed that the people all around were watching him. It made him uneasy, but he was the colonel, the man in charge. So he shrugged it off and started to inspect the body. When he looked, he looked straight into the face that stared back from the coffin with dead eyes.

The man had been placed in the box right from the battlefield. There had been no time to wedge a penny over each eye, a common practice in those days. When rigor mortis set in, there was no way to close them, so they stared out at whoever dared to invade the privacy of the coffin. To say he was shocked would be an understatement. He was downright flabbergasted to say the least.

"This couldn't be your son!" he said impulsively.

"Now why do you say that, after insisting it could be no other than our son a few minutes ago!"

The colonel bowed his head but said nothing. He looked to all around him like a small boy caught with his hand in the cookie jar. The officer coughed to clear his throat, trying to get command of the situation as he had been taught to do in officers school. He had honed his verbal skill at many a meeting with the high brass, the officers that made all the decisions for battles that they would never see, decisions that would cost thousands their lives, while the high command never had to risk their own.

But John Templer was not some pot-bellied, cigar smoking, hard drinking lady's man that, because of family ties, was now wearing a high-ranking officer's uniform. The colonel was defeated and he knew it.

There was nothing he had learned at school that would apply to this situation. He would have to humble himself. This he did graciously. Coming to his feet, he stepped around the open coffin so that he was face to face with John and his wife.

"Mr. and Mrs. Templer, I have acted in a manner unbecoming an officer of the United State Army. Please accept my apology." The officer came to attention and gave them a smart salute. "I take full responsibility for my actions. Ask of me what you will and I and my men will do our best to oblige you in tracing down your son, whether dead or alive." John gauged the man, he seemed sincere enough.

"Your apology accepted this time, colonel. But let's have no more foul ups. My wife believes our boy to be alive and I'm inclined to think so also. So my suggestion to you would be to use your considerable influence to track James down." The high-ranking soldier scratched his head for a moment thinking about what to say next.

"Rest assured we will do our best." Facing his men he ordered, "You men get this body back in the icehouse! Lieutenant! Come to my office! We need to talk." Halfway to the headquarters building, Sherman blocked their path.

"Colonel, I'm sure my uncle will be very pleased by your noble intentions." It was easy for Sherman to see the contempt the colonel and his aid had for him.

"I'm glad to hear that, Mr. Sherman. Now if you will excuse me, I'd like to get started as soon as possible" The two men sidestepped Sherman and continued into the building. Once inside the colonel closed the door and ordered the adjutant to bring a chair up close to his desk. "Those farmers really fell for that hogwash--hook, line, and sinker. Now to figure out how to get them out of our hair. Where's that hospital where they took most of the wounded from the prison camps when the war ended?"

"If my memory serves me right, it's two hundred miles southwest of here. Do you really think their boy might be there, colonel?"

"Hell, no! But it'll get them out of our hair and us out of this mess! Didn't Sherman say he was heading to the dry desert country of the Southwest for his health or something?"

“I believe that’s right, sir.”

“I want him out of here as fast as we can arrange some transportation! Get a voucher made up for three travel permits. Then have my buggy hitched up and assemble some men to escort them to the next rail line. Have the trooper in charge of the escort make sure they get on the train. I want no mistakes! We’ve had enough of them already.” The adjutant saluted and left to carry out the orders.

It took no more than ten minutes to hitch the team to the large black touring buggy, then another five minutes to get the men assembled with two days of food and water rations. The colonel had told John of his proposal to have his soldiers ride through the night as to deliver the Templers and Sherman to the nearest rail station some fifty plus miles distance from where they were now.

The two men and Ruth stepped aboard the buggy for the long ride through the night. At least it would be a comfortable ride in the colonel’s personal coach. The three agreed to leave the top down so they would not feel as closed in as the stage had felt. The buggy rode high on its oversized wheels and therefore was above the level of dust thrown by the horses as they trotted along.

Ruth fell asleep almost immediately after the buggy lurched forward. John knew she was exhausted, so he covered her with the colonel's lap blanket and let her sleep.

Doc Sherman looked over at John and said, "Why do you suppose that old bird went through all the trouble of letting us use his buggy and the like?"

"You mean having the Army pay for our tickets for as far as we want to go?" A big grin spread across Templer's face. "You know as well as I do. I think it had something to do with your uncle back at the Capital, don't you?"

Both men broke out laughing. Ruth stirred under the blanket, so the men became quiet so as not to wake her, but for the next five minutes or so a chuckle would escape from one or the other man.

After they both regained their composure, Doc Sherman leaned over toward John. "About my uncle," he said, "did you hear me say anything about my uncle being the General of the Armies?"

"Why, no, I can't rightly say I did. But I assumed by the way you were talking that it had to be the general that was your uncle."

"The truth of the matter is, I do have an Uncle William Sherman and he does have a lot of pull around Washington. The only difference is that my uncle's name is William E. Sherman and he's the ferry man!" He let out a little laugh.

"It's only a two-horse ferry across the river, so he pulls it by hand both ways. The colonel just assumed it to be the other way, my uncle being general that is! And as an old horse dealer told me once, when you assume something, you make an ass out of you and me. Get it? Ass-u-me?" Both men roared over that old joke.

Dr. Sherman told John of the Pie'ce de resistance. "Remember the big city photographer that was at the depot when we got there?"

"Yes."

"I found out he wasn't down here to glorify the big shot colonel. He only made it look that way. Said he and the colonel even made a deal about how the article was to read."

"You don't say?"

"Suckered the old man in all the way. He was really here to get anything that could be used to disgrace the old politician. Seems he works for a competitive fraction that wants the old man out to make room for one of their own people." The doctor started laughing again, "You sure gave him what he needed, and I can guarantee the colonel's not going to like what he reads."

Chapter IV

It was two weeks since John and Ruth left home in search of their oldest son James. The boys left behind had received a telegram from them saying they were going on to a hospital where they hoped to find James alive. All morning the conversation had been of hope that they would see their oldest brother alive and home once again. It was a welcome relief from the constant strain Josh felt over having killed Mr. Horstead.

Sam would sometimes have to hunt for Josh at supper time. After the first time, he knew where to look for his younger brother. Josh would be found standing in the barn staring at the spot where he pinned the old thief to the wall. He seemed to be off in another world at these times. Samuel would put his hand on his brother's shoulder and tell him it wasn't right to dwell on what he had no choice in.

"Josh, if you hadn't stopped him when you did, neither of us would be alive now. That old snake would have had to do away with Henry to boot! He couldn't leave anybody around that might have witnessed his murdering the two of us, you know." Josh would look up at his older brother and nod his head in agreement, then both of them would stroll over to the house for supper.

Still, it weighed heavily on Josh's mind and kept him from sleeping at night. It was a constant concern to his two brothers who tried to always be cheerful around him. And so it went as the days slowly moved on.

Most of the planting was done and now began the long wait before harvest time. There were chores to be sure, but these could be done in a couple of hours in the morning with only Alice to be milked in the afternoon.

Josh always seemed to be preoccupied. For a while he would join in with the other boys voicing their hopes about James being alive. Then a few days after the telegram arrived, he became more silent.

His two brothers grew more worried than ever over Josh's mood. He hadn't been himself since the incident with Horstead. They knew they had to snap him out of it before his depression grew worse. It was Henry who came up with the idea for a fishing trip.

Josh loved to fish and if anything would get him back to his old self, that would do it.

"Josh!" Sam called as his brother came out of the barn the next morning. "I've been getting a real hankering for some fresh fish. What would you say if I asked you to go catch me a dozen or so? I didn't get to do any fishin' when I was in the Army, movin' from place to place as we were. You think you could do that for me?" Josh smiled for the first time in several weeks.

"Sure, I'd be willin', but the only good fishin' hole is almost four hours walking distance. The fish would be spoiled by the time I got back, and who would do the chores tonight?"

"Don't worry about the chores, won't take me much longer to do them alone. Besides it's kind of enjoyable to do them all myself for once. Beats ridin' through the countryside all day hoping someone won't take a bead on you before sunset, then sleeping with a gun under your blanket all night. Me and the chores will get along just fine." Sam could see that Josh was getting more excited by the minute. "If you want, you can take Henry along for company."

Josh thought about that for a minute. "I think I'd like that." The problems the family was going through had matured his little brother some. "I'll go tell him to get his stuff together, but what about the fish spoiling?"

"I figure by the time you get there the fish won't be biting much, so it might be better if you camped for the night, then fished the next morning. After I get the chores done, I'll ride over and pick you and Henry up. We can eat a few fish right on the spot, then finish the rest off when we get home. Won't take long in the wagon." Josh smiled at the thought. He hadn't been fishing in a coon's age and was more than willing to get his line wet.

"Hank, hurry it up, we're goin' fishin.' It's going to be dark before you get out of the house!"

"Just hold your horses out there. I'm hurrying as fast as I can," Henry answered back. This brought a grin to Josh's face.

"Got to keep him in place," he told his older brother. A few minutes more and they were on their way across the newly planted fields. Josh was eager to get some distance behind him and the scene of his unpleasant memory. It felt good to have the sun against their backs, and they couldn't help thinking of the big fish they were sure to catch once they got settled in their camp.

"I can almost smell those fish a fryin' in the pan," Henry said while sniffing the air. Josh reached over and messed his little brother's hair.

"That's cow pies baking in the sun you're smelling."

"Maybe so, but they smell like fish a fryin' to me." With that Henry inhaled a deep breath again. "Mmm, mmm. Sure does smell good, doesn't it?" Josh smiled to himself.

"Let's get going before you go completely out of your mind."

It was early evening and Sam was out finishing the milking. Being alone, he was a little nervous about being out in the barn with just the horses and Alice for company. He knew full well that if Josh had not come to his rescue when he did, he would have been dead and buried now. Most likely his two brothers would be buried right alongside him.

Sam had forgotten how the Army had taught him to be cautious. He had been lured into the safety of the first few post war weeks; he wouldn't forget again. In his lap, within quick reach of his right hand, lay his Colt Army .44 caliber. At any unusual noise his hand would drop to his lap, and in one motion he would spin around to face any would-be opponent, gun at the ready.

Sam was just pulling the pail of warm milk from under Alice when he thought he heard a noise outside. Yes, he was sure of it now. The sound of several horses coming up the road. He blew the lamp out. Finding a spot by the door where he could not be seen, but could see anyone approaching the house, he kneeled down and waited.

The horses grew closer and Samuel could make out the outline of three riders. If they mean trouble, he thought, I'll have to pick my shots so as to get them before they can get a clear shot at me. He checked to make sure the .44 was fully loaded.

In the back of his mind, he had suspected that the killing of old man Horstead would bring more trouble down around his family's heads, and it seemed the time was at hand. Horstead was born into a large family with many kin around these parts. When one had relatives, it was only a matter of time before one of them got drunk and decided to avenge his kinsmen.

They picked a good night for it, Sam thought as he waited for them to move into the light from the house so he could get a good view of them. If it was going to be shooting they wanted, they came to the right place. Sam would keep his position, hoping for enough time for their eyes to grow accustomed to the light radiating from the window. That way, being hidden in the shadows, he would have the upper hand for at least fifteen to twenty seconds, enough time to make all the difference in the world when it was three against one.

"Ho, the house! Anybody in there?" It was the larger of the three doing the hailing.

"It's me, Vern Kelso, the sheriff. I've got the new circuit judge and my deputy with me."

"What's this all about that couldn't wait till morning, Vern?" The sheriff wheeled his horse around to face where Sam still hid in the shadows.

"That you, Sam?"

"It's me, Vern. Suppose you walk your horse over so we can talk in private." The sheriff kicked his horse into movement, reining up short of the barn door. Sam was first to speak.

"Good to see you again, Vern, but tell me what business brings you out here this time of night. Must be real important for you to ride all this way."

The sheriff looked down into the shadows trying to find Samuel in the darkness. "I tried to talk the judge out of it. Told him it could wait till morning but he would hear nothing of it. Said if I didn't want to perform my duties as appointed, he would get someone else to take my place."

"Can he do that, Vern? You've been sheriff around these parts since I was wearing diapers. Ain't heard no one complain about you yet."

"Oh, he can, and would replace me in a minute if I gave him half the chance. Anyway, the reason we're out here is to bring Josh into town for trial for the murder of old man Horstead." Sam stepped out of the doorway into the light.

"You're not serious, Vern! You know as well as I do it was a case of self-defense."

"I know that! But someone's filed charges against Josh and the judge won't listen to reason. Says I have to bring him in tonight! Sorry, Sam, but my hands are tied. I'm sure as soon as the judge hears what happened, he'll cut Josh loose and everything will be forgotten." Sam's face became drawn, his jaw set.

"Who's the person filed them charges?"

"It's Mary Jane Horstead. I don't know what she wants or hopes to gain by this, but it's all legal. You better go get Josh before the judge gets impatient and starts giving orders again. He's a real strange one, he is."

"I don't give a hoot what he is! You don't come onto a man's property to drag him off of it on the word of a little slut like Mary Jane Horstead! Besides, Josh is gone for a few days. The judge can look around to his heart's content, just keep him away from me!

"I saw his kind during the war. They live off the troubles of the innocent, hiding behind the very laws that are supposed to protect the people. They twist them all around to suit themselves. To me they're nothing but vultures."

“I heard what you said, young man!” Sam twisted his body around to meet the judge face to face.

“If you heard me then you’ll know you’re not wanted here.”

“Son, I’m a circuit judge assigned to this area, so you better mind your manners or I’ll find you in contempt of court and give you thirty days in jail!”

Sam took in a deep breath, then let it out slowly. Vern could see Sam was on the verge of exploding. “Take it easy, Sam. You could get yourself in a lot of trouble.” Sam took a step closer to the judge.

“That right? You would give me thirty days for saying my peace?”

“That’s right, son!” Sam thought about it for a minute.

“If you think your puttin’ the fear to me, you’re wrong. But if you want to try, then go right ahead. It’s your life you’re holdin’ in your hands. And I’m not your son, you highfalutin jackass.” The judge started to say something but couldn’t seem to find the words. The sheriff cut in.

“Judge, you better know. Sam here is a war hero just returned home. The people won’t like it if you throw him in jail for speakin' his mind. They'll feel you were in the wrong for coming out here at this time of night.

"In fact, if Sam shot you dead in your tracks, there wouldn't be a jury within a hundred miles that would convict him. I suggest we ride out of here while we still can. Sam will bring Josh into town when he gets back. That right, Sam?"

"That's right, Vern. Now get this poor excuse for a man out of here before I lose my temper!" The judge whirled his horse toward town and galloped off.

"That's not the last time I'll be seeing that man," Sam said to the sheriff, "but at least Josh is safe for the night."

"Good night, Sam." Vern waved as he rode after the judge.

"Good night, Vern. See what you can do about this matter, will you?" Sam watched as the trio rode off into the night.

This could turn into real trouble for Josh. Sam thought about saddling up and going out to tell Josh tonight, but then thought better of it. That judge was just angry enough to make the sheriff sit just out of sight waiting for him to make a fool move like that.

No, he would wait for morning, then take a roundabout way to the fishin' hole, only heading for it when he was sure he wasn't being followed. Sam figured he better turn in so he could get an early start.

An hour before sunup, Sam went out and did the chores, then started to hitch the team to the spring wagon, but decided instead to take his stallion and trail the gelding behind for Josh and Henry to ride. It wasn't uncommon to see a rider trailing another horse behind him, so Sam knew he wouldn't bring much attention to himself. Trailing two horses would be a different story.

Before Sam led the horses from the barn, he climbed the ladder to the hayloft. Using his Army telescope, he glassed the surrounding countryside to make sure there were no riders standing off in the distance. Seeing none, he climbed back down the ladder to where the horses were waiting. One last look around and he mounted his great stallion. Taking the reins to the gelding he galloped out the back gate, looking over his shoulder every so often to see if anyone followed.

While he was riding, he crossed some fresh tracks in the soft dirt surrounding the newly plowed field. They were going in the same direction he was. Sam stopped his horse to examine the marks in the soil. Was someone waiting just beyond the rise? He looked to the top of the hill to see if he could pick up any outline that didn't fit in with its surroundings. All seemed clear so he rode on.

After a while he slowed the horses to an easier pace, one that could be maintained without tiring the animals, just in case he spotted someone coming up fast behind. If that happened he could always get out of sight into the cluster of scrub oak, then spur the horses on to put as much distance between him and the pursuer as he could.

It was nearly eight in the morning when Sam arrived at the fishing hole. He hadn't been here in some time, but it still looked the same as the last time he was here. The same wide, sparkling creek with the small waterfall just to the north. To the south was a large stand of evergreens, uncommon in these parts. Probably planted by some homesteader years before.

In a sandy part along the creek were Josh and Henry's bedrolls all rolled out like they had just been placed there. Josh and Henry were nowhere to be seen. Sam did see something else though, the same hoof prints as he had seen before. He could tell from a chip out of the left rear shoe. It showed wherever the horse stepped in soft dirt.

Sam jerked his .44 out of the holster, then dismounted. Pushing the pistol inside his coat to keep it from sight, he led the two horses over to a small bush where he tied their reins.

"Hi, Sam." The voice came from down the creek about a dozen yards. It was Henry. Sam waved back, feeling more at ease now that he knew the boys were all right. But who was the rider that passed through here not more than an hour ahead of him?

Sam had an uneasy feeling, and it was getting stronger. By now Henry had come up along side him. He held a nice string of fish.

"Ready for some good eatin', Sam?"

Sure am! Nice fish you got there, brother. Where's Josh hiding out?"

"He's just beyond that clump of trees, doesn't know you're here yet, I guess."

"Well, get those critters ready for the frying pan and I'll go get him." Sam pushed his way through some low brush between the trees. He was just about to step into the open when he was brought up short. There on the bank with his back toward Sam was a large man, fishing pole in hand. Sam watched for a moment.

"Hi, Sam. Come on over and get yourself a fishin' pole."

Sam kept his eye on the man; he still held his .44 in his jacket out of sight. There was something familiar about the man sitting there across from Josh. The man put his pole on the ground beside him and got up, still keeping his back to Sam. I know that hulk from somewhere, Sam thought. He walked around the man.

"Hi ya, Sam. What took you so long? We were going to eat without you if you didn't show soon." The large hulk of a man was no other than Vern Kelso, the sheriff. He had a large grin on this face.

"What the heck you doin' out here, Vern?"

The sheriff stopped smiling for a moment, then stepped forward. “Can I talk to you in private, Sam?”

Sam looked at the seriousness on his friend’s face, then motioned Vern to follow him over to a grassy spot along the bank.

“What you got on your mind?” he asked the sheriff. “It has to do with Josh, doesn’t it?”

Kelso took out a plug of chewing tobacco. “Have a chew of tobacco, Sam?” The sheriff held out the plug to Sam. Sam tore off a piece and placed it between his teeth and gums.

“Not what’s this about, Vern?” Vern looked around, then finding a soft spot in the grass settled into it.

“Sam, there’s trouble in town over this affair with Josh and old man Horstead. The judge was so mad last night when we got into town, that he wanted to form a posse to hunt Josh down like he was a common killer.”

“He wanted to do what?”

“That crazy bastard started knocking on doors trying to get enough men together. The only ones wantin’ to go were a few drunks and some of the

Horstead kin. They had blood in their eye, so I figured I'd better ride out to protect the boy. Would have stopped to get you, but thought you might fly off the handle and shoot one of them. You understand, don't you?" Vern waited for Sam to speak.

"How'd you know where Josh was? I didn't mention anything."

"You forget. I'm Josh's godfather. Me and him been fishin' this same spot ever since he was in knee pants. I'm the one who showed him this place, remember?" Vern smiled one of his big toothy smiles.

"Did the judge get a posse together?"

"Like I said, he got a few, all of them riffraff. You know the kind, good for nothing. I didn't like what I saw, so I gave a few dollars to Jeb Anderson and told him to set 'em up at the bar. Worked like a charm. Within a few minutes, with all the free whiskey they could drink, no one was willin' to ride out after anybody. Even the Horstead bunch was more interested in gettin' a free drunk than going out after Josh."

"What did the judge do about that?"

"Hell, that old buzzard was doing most of the drinking! He'll stay out of our hair until he sobers up, and that won't be for a few days." Vern laughed, "I sent a bottle up to his room, anonymously, of course." Sam chuckled at what Vern had done.

"Hey, you guys! Going to eat some fish or hold hands instead?" Vern picked up a clump of dirt and threw it at Josh. "I hope you got a lot of them. Your big brother here looks a might hungry if you ask me." Almost immediately a dozen or more fish landed in Vern's lap. They were still wet from the creek.

"That enough for ya or do ya want more?" Vern's eyes followed up the string to where it fastened to Henry's pole. As he reached the tip of it, Henry stepped back while at the same time jerking the fishing pole overhead.

"Watch out!" Sam yelled, but too late. The fish slammed into Vern's face. Now everybody was laughing. When Vern got back to his feet, he looked as though he had wet his pants. Henry told him so.

"I guess you got me too excited. I just couldn't hold it any more." Vern laughed.

It wasn't long before the fishermen had all the fish they wanted for the day. After eating their fill of golden brown trout, they laid back and contemplated their full stomachs, no one wanting to disturb the peace and harmony of the other. Sam lay propped up on one elbow, the coming trouble weighing heavily on his mind. He wanted to tell his little brother, but Josh looked so happy at the moment he didn't want to break the spell.

Vern seemed to sense what was on Sam's mind. "It can wait," he whispered to Sam. "You can tell him when you bring him into town in a few days after everything's quieted down a bit."

Sam shook his head, then laid back resting his head in his hands. "Sure is peaceful out here," he said. He was soon fast asleep.

The sun was high overhead when the group started back to the farm. Vern was going to ride escort on the way back just in case the judge or anyone else got any more crazy ideas. He really didn't expect any, but thought he better be sure. It would be an easy ride with the two boys on the one horse and Vern and Sam on their own.

While they rode Vern kept an eye out for any trouble that might be headed their way. Something inside was bothering him, he didn't know what, just sensed something was wrong.

A short distance from where they rode stood a large stand of trees with low laying brush around their base. Once past this last grove of trees and they would have a clear view of any riders for miles around.

The trees looked so inviting and cool that they decided to stop and give the horses a rest out of the hot sun. There was an animal trail to one side of the grove wandering out of sight deep within the miniature forest. To this they rode, seeking shade enough for all. Coming upon a small area where the trees were spaced some distance apart, but whose branches formed an interwoven cover high overhead, they reined to a halt and dismounted.

"Looks like someone's already been here today." Vern was pointing to some tracks by the edge of the path. "I'd say three or four of them, maybe more. Don't know how they could have gotten out of here without us seeing them.

Sam bent down to look at the prints in the dirt. He pulled up a piece of grass and examined it carefully, "Maybe they're over at the water hole watering their horses and resting like we're doing."

"I doubt it, that old watering hole dried up a couple summers ago. Ain't been water here since."

Vern was getting nervous. Things didn't feel right, and with all the ex-soldiers coming back from the battlefields, no tellin' who might be passin' through. There was news from further south about a hard bunch looting, raping, and killing as they went. Never could tell, but they might decide to head north. Vern relayed his thoughts to Sam.

"I've had the same feelin' myself ever since we rode in here. Maybe it's best we ride back out quick." Josh and Henry were listening to the conversation, so when Sam motioned them to mount up, they were ready. Josh swung easily into the saddle and reached down to help Henry up behind him.

Instead of clasping Henry's hand, his extended figure went up to his mouth in a signal for everyone to be still. Was it just his imagination or had he seen an out of place shadow back in the trees? Keeping in the same position, he scanned over the surrounding brush, the shadow was gone. In its place a man was crouched behind some brush. The man had a rifle across his lap! Josh pulled his foot over the saddle horn and slid to the ground beside Henry.

What's up, Josh?" Henry asked.

Before Josh could answer, a bullet smashed into the saddle horn where Josh's leg had been moments before.

"Hit the dirt!" someone yelled.

In the open meadow there wasn't much cover. By laying flat on their bellies, the same bushes that hid the killers would also hide the sheriff's party from being easy targets. And it would force the ambushers to come from their hiding places to be able to get a clear shot.

Sam and the sheriff had drawn their guns at the very first shot and were now waiting for the attackers to give their positions away. The wait was short. Sam saw him first. A burly man with a sawed-off double barrel shotgun was trying to keep under cover while he crept forward for a better shot. Sam leveled his gun so the sights lined up on the man's chest. There was a small tree between Sam and his target, and behind this the man withdrew before Sam could pull the trigger.

Henry had thrown himself flat next to Sam, and was visibly scared. Again the man showed, this time he held the shotgun in front of him ready for use. Sam took careful aim, then squeezed the trigger. The man jerked upright, but remained on his feet. Sam looked into the man's eyes. There was not the terror one would expect to see in the eyes of a mortally wounded man such as this one. Only rage showed.

Sam took careful aim and pulled off another shot, aiming slightly to the left of where the first projectile hit. The .44 caliber bullet slammed into the man's chest. It didn't even phase him. The man took a few steps forward, then raised the shotgun to his shoulder. Sam had never known a man to continue an attack with two .44's in him.

The shotgun was pointed right at Sam and the man was pulling back on the trigger. To Sam, everything seemed to be in slow motion. It almost seemed impossible to lift his own gun to fire again, but he must. He had to stop this devil now or it would be too late.

The sheer power of the man seemed to take control of Sam, leaving him weak and defenseless. Sam knew he was about to die. Then the gunman suddenly twisted in an unearthly move, his shotgun going off at the same time. Sam could feel the concussion from the blast. Dirt was thrown up in his face, but through it all he could see the man's face disintegrate as he fell backwards, the second barrel going off into the air.

A moan brought Sam back to reality. Henry lay in a pool of blood, his right arm torn off a few inches below the shoulder.

"Oh my, God!" Sam screamed. Henry hadn't even been wearing a gun, and now here he was with his life's blood draining out of him onto the ground. Quickly Sam tore his belt loose and placed it around Henry's stump of an arm. After putting a stick through the belt he twisted, tightening the loop around Henry's injured arm until the flow of blood stopped.

Sporadic firing kept going on around him as he leaned over Henry keeping the tourniquet tight. To his right he could see Josh edged up against a rotten stump from a tree cut years ago. Vern had moved closer to the line of brush and was returning shots in the direction where most of the firing was coming from. Every time Vern fired a round, it would be answered with at least five others.

With Sam working to save Henry's life and unable to help, the burden fell on Vern's shoulders. The odds against them were high. Vern had no illusions about that. Their only hope was if they could hold their ground, then slip away when it got dark. There wasn't much chance of that with darkness still over seven hours away.

"Vern, give me a gun!" Josh knew Vern kept one in his boot and, if he could get to it, Josh had a plan on how he might use it to get them out of this mess.

"Here, but it won't do much good against the odds we're up against, it's only a .32 caliber." He threw it to Josh a few feet away.

In an instant Josh checked it, then pushed it into his belt. Keeping low, he then pulled his boots off. On Vern's next shot he ran as fast as he could back down the trail away from the ambush area.

In the background he could hear several startled cries, then a few bullets flew past him. He dove for the cover of a fallen tree, then lay still, listening. He expected someone at any moment to come out of the bushes in search of him.

No one came. They must've figured they could catch him in the fields at will after they did away with the business at hand. It was the edge Josh was hoping for, and he took no time in putting it to his advantage. Gathering his breath and keeping low, he stayed just inside the outer rim of trees and brush.

This way if one of the gang members decided to come looking for him, he could just drop to the ground and let the would-be murderers ride past before they saw him. He kept moving through the brush stopping every few seconds to listen for anyone approaching him.

From the firing going on in the trees, Josh knew that he would have to act fast or there would be no hope for the rest of his group. Then it would be just a matter of time before they hunted him down and killed him where they found him.

Judging from the sun he was just about behind the ambushers. Now Josh could only wait. During each volley of shots he would move closer to where he knew the killers would be well hidden--hidden from their intended victims, but not, he hoped, from someone coming up behind them.

They might have one man guarding the horses. He would probably also be watching the fields for any riders coming this way. Little chance of that! The nearest farm was over five miles away and the wind was blowing away from that direction, carrying the sound of gun shots with it. There would be no riders coming to the rescue. Josh knew it and they would know it too!

A horse snorted somewhere close by. Josh dropped to the ground, the pistol pointing in the direction of the sound. Raising his head, he could barely make out the shape of a horse's rear. If a guard was with them, he was keeping out of sight.

Josh crawled toward some tangled brush off to his left. From there he would be able to get a better view and hopefully be able to see if anybody was posted as a lookout. Finding a small opening in the bushes where a small animal ate while bedding down, he quickly crawled into this spot.

From here he could see that the horses were saddled, but all had been hobbled to keep them from bolting at the first sound of gunfire. Josh looked the area over carefully until he was sure they were not being watched. If he could take the hobbles off and run them off, his brothers and the sheriff might have a chance to escape.

Worming his way out of the den, he gained his feet and ran to the first horse. It wouldn't take long to set all the horses free, all he would need is a few minutes. The first knot came loose easily in his hands. He thought about shooing each horse in turn as he untied them but thought better of it, realizing they still offered cover while he worked at untying the rest of the mounts.

"Hold it right where you're at!" The words rang like an explosion in Josh's ears. "Get up real slow and turn around so I can see you!" Josh did as he was told.

The man had come up unnoticed behind Josh, as he was intent on turning the horses loose. Josh knew it wouldn't do any good to try to talk his way out of this, the situation called for action.

"You're just a boy!" the man growled. "The men too scared to do the dirty work so they sent you?" Josh didn't speak, he just stood there motionless.

"Boy, you're going to retie those horses, then me and you are going to take a walk."

"Walk where?" Josh asked, trying to throw the man off guard.

"Just keep your yap shut and start hobbling that horse!"

Josh kept still, wondering why the man hadn't noticed the revolver in his belt. Josh stole a glance downward. While making his way through the brush, his shirt had been pulled out. It now hid the gun from sight. The man moved in closer to make his point, shoving the rifle he was carrying into Josh's stomach just missing the hidden pistol. He warned Josh to get a move on or he would shoot him on the spot. Josh took a step backward then stopped. The man shoved the rifle barrel at Josh's midsection again, but this time Josh's left hand thrust out and pushed the barrel to the side.

A look of astonishment spread across the man's face as he tried to realign the barrel towards Josh. It was no use! Before the stranger knew what happened, Josh's right hand retrieved the .32 from his belt. In one quick motion he brought it up and pulled the trigger.

The man and boy stood facing each other for what seemed like an eternity. Josh felt that he must have missed the man altogether. As the smoke from Josh's gun cleared, he could see a small round dot of red on the man's forehead, no dripping blood, just a small round spot of red.

"Give me your rifle!" Josh commanded the bandit, then pulled it from the dying man's fingers. The man took a few steps back as if trying to get away, then slowly sank to the ground, the little round hole now dribbling blood down the face of the man who lay still on the ground. Reaching down Josh unbuckled the man's gun belt. The man's handgun was another 32 like the one Josh carried, but his rifle was a new Spencer lever gun in 52 caliber with brass cartridges. Josh searched the man for more ammunition, figuring he might need the extra ammo for the gun.

He glanced over his shoulder at the horses. Four of them. That means unless Vern got a lucky shot, there were still two left. Josh took stock of the situation. He was in the middle of a small clearing ringed by trees and waist-high brush. To his left was a narrow path, probably made by deer. In front of him the dead man lay, and to his right the horses grazed as if still hobbled.

Where would the men come from when they came to get their horses? The brush was so thick along the edge of the clearing that it would be almost impossible for a man to get through without being scratched to the bone.

Why was the brush so thick around the edge, Josh wondered. Of course, before it had dried up several years before, a water hole had been in this very spot. The path had been worn in by animals coming down to drink. Now Josh knew that the only way a man could come through here was by the path and the path alone.

Josh found a place to conceal himself from sight, a place that would give him a clear view of the dried pond but would hide him from anyone coming along the path. He checked the rifle, it had four bullets in it. He pulled six more rounds from the gun belt and loaded them into the rifle.

He was now set for what had to be done. Cupping his hands he yelled as loud as he could. "Riders coming! Riders coming! Let's get the hell out of here!" Then he waited.

Didn't take more than a few seconds before he heard them coming, two men on a dead run. Even from a hundred feet away he could tell they were already winded, huffing as they were for breath. He knew they would burst out into the opening, out of breath and not expecting any trouble to be this close at hand. They'd be lookin' towards the fields trying to see how much time they had to make their getaway.

They ran right past Josh, one man in front of the other. Upon seeing the body of their companion, they both dropped to a squatting position, their backs making broad targets for Josh.

"I'm behind you, you bastards!" Josh held the lever action rifle to his side not worrying about aiming. At this range it would be near impossible to miss. One man flung himself around. The bullet from Josh's rifle caught him in the neck, breaking it instantly. Josh levered another round into the chamber, but to his surprise the second man raised his hands.

"I give up! I give up!" he yelled. Josh thought about shooting him in the back, but didn't.

"Turn around," he ordered the man. The man turned to face Josh.

"You're not going to kill me, I know your kind. Can't kill a man that's not armed."

"You got a gun in your holster."

"That don't make no difference! I'd let you go if things was changed around," he grinned. "So, I'm going to back over to my horse and just ride out of here, won't be any bother to you none."

Josh glared back at the man. "Who sent you, mister?"

"Why the judge, boy. The judge, that's who." The man smiled, sure of his escape.

"You don't know me, mister!" Josh said. "And you're not going anywhere but jail."

The killer stopped, still grinning. "Why would you want to take me to jail, sonny? The judge would just turn me loose anyway."

He took his hat off and wiped his forehead with the sleeve of his arm, then started to put it back on but seemed to think better of it. The man and the boy stood there facing each other for a long moment. Then for no apparent reason Josh raised his gun and shot the man in the chest. The man stumbled forward toward Josh, then collapsed at his feet. Josh bent down and turned the man over.

"How'd you know?" the man whispered.

"I heard the click!"

"Killed by a click," the man said as his eyes closed. Josh picked up the dead man's hat. As he did so a small .44 Derringer fell out. It was cocked, ready to fire. Josh let the hammer down then cocked it again. Yes, it was the gun being cocked that he had heard.

Henry was unconscious from lack of blood, and there would be a long ride to the nearest doctor. It was obvious he could not ride sitting up, so a sling was made from two long poles with rope strung in a lace-work pattern between them to support Henry's body. By placing a horse at each end, Henry could be carried lying down.

The going was rough and Henry would let out little involuntary moans with each step of the horses. Josh had gathered the killers' horses and was trailing them behind him. The plan was to carry the stretcher at a fast trot until the horses tired, then replace them with the fresh mounts. It was easy to see after the first few minutes that it would be impossible to go at more than a slow walk.

Time was running out for Henry and everyone knew it. Sam knew enough from watching the doctors on the battlefields to stop and loosen the tourniquet every few minutes. "Henry needs help bad!" Sam looked up at Josh. Nothing else had to be said.

Josh dropped the reins of two of the horses, then wrapped the other pair around his left hand. Whipping his stead into action, he raced off at a full run. His plan was to ride the first horse until it tired, switch to the second, then the third, riding it into the ground if he had to. He hadn't gone far when in the distance he saw riders coming hard. His first thought was to change direction and try to outrun them. Trouble was they were between him and Doc Bantly's place, and without a doctor, Henry didn't have a chance.

One rider stood out from the others, something about the way he sat on a horse, rider and horse seemed as one. That rider could only be Ben Riehl. It was too good to be true. Josh was out of breath when he got to

Ben, but by using hand language to fill in, he relayed what had happened.

Ben took charge, first sending Josh on his way to Doc's place to get things ready for Henry's arrival. Next he sent another man to Tom Homan's farm to get several coils of rope. After getting the rope, he would ride at a fast clip to another rider waiting halfway between where they figured Sam's party to be. This rider would bring the rope the rest of the way. Ben and the others rode on to meet Sam.

Henry was in bad shape when Ben reached him, the party having only gone a little over a mile from the scene of the ambush. Until the ropes arrived there was nothing Ben could do but ride alongside Henry, occasionally leaning over and wiping Henry's face with a wet kerchief.

Where was that rope? The thought went through Ben's mind. What if there wasn't anyone at the Homan's place? They were farmers, not ranchers like Ben had been before moving out here. He said a silent prayer, a prayer that had to be answered if the boy was to live.

A lone rider showed in the distance. Squinting, Ben could see the rider holding several coils of rope as he rode hell-bent for leather towards them. Ben rode to meet the man, then returned with the rope.

Quickly he tied a loop in the ends of the ropes, then cut these in ten-foot lengths. Doing the same with the rest of the ropes he now had four pieces of rope with a small loop at the ends. Sam and Vern eyed him but didn't say anything. Ben was a man known for using his head when things got tough and always coming up with the right thing at the right time.

"You men do as I told you. Now all together, let's go." Ben had briefed them on the way over. The men slid from their saddles as Ben had Sam bring his horse to a stop. Each man went to the end of a pole and lifted it, untying the short pieces of rope Sam had placed on them. These they replaced with the ropes Ben had prepared. Now the stretcher was suspended solely by the four ten-foot ropes.

"Sam, you and Vern hold the stretcher up while the men mount their horses." As soon as the men mounted up, they tied the ends of their ropes around their saddle horns. The stretcher was now suspended between four horses instead of two.

"Each man grab the rope in your hands to act as a buffer. Remember, keep your horses in step with the other! Now, let's get this boy to some help!" It was quite a sight to see the four horsemen riding along at a fast trot, stretcher gliding smoothly along between them. On it, a ten-year old boy was fighting for his life.

Henry fought hard to live. If not for the fast thinking of Ben Riehl, his chance for life would have been gone. Now laying in Doc Bantly's back bedroom, feverish and weak from the lack of blood, the boy showed the strong stock he was made of. It would be touch and go for a few weeks, but except for his arm, Henry would recover.

Sam wasn't sure about Josh's recovery though. He had sent him fishing to help forget about old man Horstead. Now Josh was forced to kill two more men. From farm boy to killer, all in less than two weeks. What would the folks think? What must Josh feel? He had been thrust into manhood faster than any child should be with no choice in the matter. To survive or die were the only choices Josh had. Sam felt a growing anger well up from deep within.

Chapter IX

The mansion stood at the top of a little knoll overlooking the wide river before it. Magnolia trees spread their lofty limbs in graceful welcome to all who would come before them. White pillars reached from the bluest of skies to the plush green lawn at their base. A wide porch made of red brick lay behind them edging up to the main structure of white hand-planed boards.

In the center a wide door of oak split down the middle, both halves opening inward to the heart of this magnificent mansion. A small neatly-lettered sign gave notice to strangers. It read: "Give us your sick, your wounded. In return we give you hope."

John turned to the man who had brought them here. "You sure this is the hospital?" Eyes flickered from under a hat brim faded from years in the sun.

"Yes, sir, this is the hospital all right."

John asked the man again, "You sure?" This time the man just nodded.

"Honey, you wait here and I'll see what's going on. Sure don't look like no hospital to me." On John's second knock, the door opened and before John stood a black, immaculately dressed male servant.

"Yes, sir, may I help you?"

John was taken aback. Now he was sure they had come to the wrong place. Boy, would he give a piece of his mind to the driver. Was it some kind of joke the man was playing, or was the man slow in the mind and really thought this was a hospital?

"Excuse me. We were on our way to the hospital where the war wounded were being treated, and the man that is driving us swore this was the place."

"He is correct, sir," the man said. "I see that your wife is with you. Will you please both come in? Miss Jamie will see you presently."

John motioned for Ruth to join him. The servant led them into a luxuriously appointed library where he requested them to be seated.

"May I offer you a drink? We don't have much in the way of liqueurs, but we still have some fine wine available in our wine cellar."

John refused, saying that he couldn't drink their private stock. After all, he and Ruth were strangers here.

The man offered the drink again saying, "Sir, to Miss Jamie there are no strangers, just friends whom she hasn't yet met."

Ruth was still awestruck from this paradise amongst the ruin of the countryside around them. "How far is the hospital from here? I judge it must be upon the plantation grounds."

"I will be glad to show you there myself, but first I must know something about you and who it is you are looking for." The Templers were not prepared for the lady that was now speaking to them from the stairway.

To Ruth she looked as if she was going to a grand ball. To John she was a vision from a dream--the type of woman all men secretly desire, yet are afraid to hold close for fear she will steal their very soul away.

"Miss Jamie, may I present the Templers. They are here in search of their son who was in the Union Army."

The woman crossed the room to where the Templers sat. On her approach John stood to show respect, while Ruth not knowing what to do, stood up beside him. It was unnerving what a beautiful woman could do to those in her presence, be it man or woman.

"You are here to find your son?"

"Yes, he was an artillery officer with the Union Army."

"Why do you think he might be here? Do you have some reason to believe he was wounded around here?"

John shuffled his feet, unable to look the woman straight in the eye. She waited for him to answer. "We were told by Colonel Pelky that he may be here."

The lady saw the uneasiness in John and asked him to be seated and tell her the whole story. "But first," she said, "have some wine and cookies. It will help you relax."

The wine more than relaxed John; he had to fight to stay awake. It had been a hard trip with not much chance for rest, and John was showing the results of it now. It was embarrassing sitting here in front of the most beautiful woman he had ever seen in his life, and it was all he could do to stay awake.

"Please excuse me, I think I could use some air." With that John walked out to the front porch. It was several minutes before his head cleared enough to go back inside.

In his absence, Ruth had told the story of how she and John had come this far in search of their oldest son. Miss Jamie asked questions from time to time until she had a clear description in her mind of what James looked and acted like.

"As I was saying to your wife, Mr. Templer, I'm sure your son is not here at this time. Although there is the distinct possibility he was here up until two weeks ago. Yes, I'm almost sure it was him." She smiled at John.

"Let me ask one of the men in the hospital. He would know for sure. He was close with your son, if it is your son who was here. It will not take but a minute to be sure. Please make yourself comfortable. I shall be right back."

"May we go with you? We have to be sure. We have come such a long way."

"Mr. Templer, I have no objections to you coming. But it is not a pretty sight for a woman to see. Men are dying every day, some out of their heads with pain. I would deeply recommend that Mrs. Templer stay here while I find out if it is indeed your son. If he's already gone, it's no use you going through any more than you have to. Do you mind waiting here for me?"

Ruth eyed the red-headed woman for a moment then agreed that it might be best.

"Stevens," Miss Jamie called. The servant entered.

"Yes, ma'am?"

"Please show Mrs. Templer where she can freshen up. I and Mr. Templer will be in back seeking the whereabouts of their son."

"Yes, ma'am. Will you please follow me, ma'am?" John waited while the servant led Ruth from the room.

"Now, Mr. Templer, the hospital's through this door."

It was the smell that hit John full in the face that was the most shocking. In the space of a wall, the scene changed from one of culture and luxury with the smell of peach blossoms in the air to the stink and horror of the sick and dying, the wounded and the dead.

Piles of gray and blue in the corner, wall-to-wall cots lining one room with only enough space to walk between. On these cots lay men in all stages of life. Some being given water and food while others, held in the hands of the nurses who attended them, were beyond the need for anything but a kind prayer to help them on their way to heaven or maybe hell.

The whole place became silent when Miss Jamie walked in. Walking through the rolls of human debris, a hand would reach out toward them, and Miss Jamie would take it in her own as if it belonged to a favored suitor instead of a wretched wreck of human flesh.

They came to a cot where a man sat, his head wrapped in blood-stained bandages.

"George, this is Mr. Templer. He's here to find out about his son, James. I told him you might be able to clarify whether your friend was his son or not. Would you mind talking to him?"

"No, Missy, I will talk to him."

Miss Jamie thanked him, then explained to John that the man had come to America from Sweden a year before the war started, so it may be a little difficult to understand him at times.

George, hearing her, told John with a grin, "I'll take my time in speaking so you know what I say."

"Do you know this man?" John asked, showing the man a tintype of the Templer family and pointing to James.

"Ya, I know him, he my friend. He stay with me when I have fever. But he go now."

John felt excitement growing within. "Where? Where has he gone now?"

The soldier scratched his head, then felt the bandaged area. He looked to see if there was fresh blood on his hand. Satisfied, he waved to the northwest.

"He go to Jolly Creek. Take food and medicine to camp. No one go, so he go! Say people die, no food, no medicine. Ya, he go to Jolly Creek Camp. You go, you find him there."

The man reached for his bandage again, then looked off in a sort of daze. John tried to thank him, but the man had drifted to a world of his own and did not hear.

Miss Jamie returned to John's side. "Did you find out anything that might help you?"

"Do you know of a place called Jolly Creek or Jolly Camp somewhere to the northwest of here?" There was excitement in John's voice.

Miss Jamie took a hard look at John, then asked why he was interested in Jolly Creek Camp.

"He says James went there with supplies for the camp. He said no one else would go, so James went. Why would that be so? Why wouldn't anyone take supplies to a camp?"

"Come with me, Mr. Templer. I think I can explain everything." She led him into the library where Ruth sat waiting. "I'm afraid I may have some distressing news for you if what George says is right. Jolly Creek Camp is having a problem right now, and your son may have walked into something he may not be able to come back from."

"Ma'am, I don't want to be rude, but what are you talking about? You tell us our son was here, then left, and how he's in some kind of trouble." John was getting irritated and it showed.

Miss Jamie remained calm and collected, her breeding evident. This irritated John all the more.

"Mr. Templer," she said, "the camp at Jolly Creek is in the midst of a smallpox epidemic! If your son went there, he may be beyond help. They have guards on the roads to keep anyone from leaving. When he bought supplies in town I thought he was heading for the gold fields. Many men are, you know."

"James bought supplies and you thought he was going to the gold fields? Ma'am, I don't doubt you, but it isn't like James to go off without at least writing us a letter, especially when he's been gone so long from home. Ma'am, beg your pardon, but it's hard to believe he'd do that."

The lady took a deep breath. "Mr. Templer, I saw you show a picture to George. Was it of your son?"

John took the picture from his pocket without saying anything and handed it to her. "It's of the whole family. James is second from the right."

The woman looked at the picture closely, then gave it back. "Yes, your son was here. He's a little older now, of course, but I am certain it is he."

John gave a quick glance at Ruth. "Could that soldier be right about James going up to the camp with the smallpox? He didn't appear to be all here, probably cause of his wound."

"Mr. Templer, if George said that's where your son went, you can be sure that's where you'll find your son if he made it that far! George only looks like he's out of his mind. He just does that when the pain gets too great.

"He told me once that he imagines himself as a young boy playing in the fields of home. He tries to remember what everything smelled and felt like, and while he's doing this, the pain becomes less and less." Miss Jamie closed the door behind them. "You can believe what he told you."

"Then I must go up there immediately. Is there a place where I can buy or rent a horse?"

Miss Jamie looked at John curiously. She could see it would do no good to try to talk him out of going. "There's a stable out back of the house with seven horses in it. You may take your pick of any of them, on the condition that you allow your wife to stay here and rest.

"As I said before, there are men guarding the only road into Jolly Creek, and they may give you a rough time. It would be no place for a woman." John agreed, then went out to the stable to pick out a horse.

While he was in the barn Stevens came out. "Master Templer, Miss Jamie asked me to give you this." He handed John a Colt Army model .44 with a holster and belt to go with it. "She said you may need it." Along with the gun Stevens handed John a small box tied with string. "Food!" he said, then left John to his work.

Chapter X

Jolly Creek Camp had originally been a stopover for cattlemen driving herds into Mexico. As of late, it was used by prospectors going west to the gold fields and now was the home to about twenty squatters trying to make a living off the land with five hundred sheep. Everything had been going well for the settlers until the outbreak of smallpox.

The contagious disease might have spread had it not been for word getting out through a drifter who happened to get wind of it while passing through the Jolly Creek area. Soon the farmers and ranchers took the initiative and closed off the area, allowing no one to enter or leave. Suspecting the sheep to be carriers of the disease they shot or by other means killed the complete flock.

Those settlers that were not ill with smallpox were soon on the verge of starvation with little food. And to make matters worse, a couple of rogues were hired to make sure the quarantine was enforced. These were brutish men caring not for anyone but themselves.

From the high ground where they camped, they had a commanding view of the camp. Anyone trying to leave would be within easy rifle shot, and these men were not afraid to kill anyone trying to escape. They were hired killers paid to do just that if need be, and they liked to kill.

When James, recuperating from his wounds, heard of the plight of these unfortunate souls, he knew he had to do something to help. So taking his Army pay, he caught a ride to the nearest settlement to buy a wagon and supplies.

Along with the necessities of food and medicine, he also bought a cask of rotgut whiskey. James had a plan and the whiskey would play an integral part in it. While in town he also made sure to write his folks and let them know he was all right, his wound keeping him from this duty until now.

James waited for night to fall before hitching the team. When it was dark enough, he walked down the main street of the settlement, making sure no suspicious person was about to give word of his departure.

Further down the street three riders pulled up in front of the saloon, stepped down, and went in. A storekeeper swept the boardwalk in front of the store, giving James a casual look now and then.

Was the storekeeper watching him or was James just too overly cautious? James found a chair in front of the saloon and sat down. Out of his pocket he pulled a piece of jerky and began to chew it. Finishing this, he leaned the chair back against the wall, put his feet up on the hitching rail and pulled his hat down over his eyes to nap. At least that's what he hoped the storekeeper would think.

The storekeeper took one last look in James' direction, then went inside locking the door behind him. James didn't move and, sure enough, the man checked one more time before being satisfied that James was as he seemed--just a man taking a nap.

Most of the people lived in back of their stores or in houses a few hundred feet behind the main street, leaving the street itself dark and deserted except for the occasional drunk coming from the saloon.

A half moon was just showing from behind a few scattered clouds when James drove out of town, keeping the horses at a slow walk so as not to be heard. Jolly Creek Camp was only a couple hours out and

James covered the distance without seeing another rider. He doubted whether he had been spotted leaving, as anyone wishing to warn the sentinels would have to use the same road that he was on.

James was wondering if he had taken the wrong road when a voice came out of the darkness. "Pull that wagon up right there, mister!" James did as he was told.

"Now get down, keepin' your hands where we can see 'em!" James had expected this and made no big fuss over it.

"What you got in that wagon?" the voice asked. James reached down and pulled the tarp back, making sure not to make any threatening moves with his hands.

"Just supplies as you can see." A man came out of the darkness, he was big and mean looking and smelled foul. A five-day growth of beard showed on his face.

"Tryin' to sneak supplies into the camp are you." It was more of a statement than a question. James smiled at the man.

"Sneak into camp? Why would I want to sneak into camp?"

A second man came into view, this one smaller and bald-headed. He reminded James of a rat. "You tellin' us you wasn't sneakin' into the camp with all those supplies?"

Again James asked why would he be sneaking into camp.

"The sickness!"

James looked puzzled. "What sickness?"

"The pox. You know, the smallpox!" James looked surprised.

"You mean to tell me there's smallpox down there?"

The little man gave James a sideways look. "If you didn't know about it, why you coming at night?"

"It's cooler, I'm not from around here, so it's easier for me to travel by night. Can't stand the heat!"

The smaller man looked at James with a look of distrust. "Then how come all them supplies? You goin' to tell me you're a big eater and need all that food for yourself?"

James looked straight at the man. "No, I'm bringing it to the camp." The Rat took his hat off and threw it on the ground.

"I just asked you if you was takin' that food to the camp and you said you weren't! Now you says you are! What you tryin' to pull? You take me for some kind of a jackass?" A rat, James thought, but kept it to himself.

"You asked me why I was sneaking into the camp. I said I wasn't sneaking any place. I didn't say I wasn't going into camp."

The rat was getting madder by the minute while the bigger man watched, saying nothing. It was plain to see he had been lost the first few moments of the conversation.

"Well, what is it then? Are ya takin' them supplies to camp or ain't ya?"

"I am taking them to camp, but I'm not sneaking them to camp!" The big man started laughing at the rat's frustration.

"You ain't takin' no supplies to Jolly Camp, we're here to see to that! You might as well turn the wagon around and hightail it out of here," the rat ordered. "But first let's see what you got in there we can use."

James smiled a knowing smile to the big man. James didn't protest, just said, "Help yourself, makes no difference to me. They already paid for it."

The men pulled lids off boxes, poked a dirty finger here and there, all the time eyeing the cask of rot gut. The rat wasn't sure if James would put up a fight, so was taking it slow and easy.

"See anything you gents want, it's on the house. Or maybe I should say on those people down there," he laughed. "There's a cask of rotgut in the back there, hard to see in this light." James knew they had spotted it first off. "Sure keeps a man company on a lonely night like this. Help yourself, gents." The two men hauled the cask out of the wagon and carried it to their camp.

"Here, I think there's some tin cups in here somewhere."

"Watch him, Al, he might have a gun in there!" The big man sprang to his feet, rifle at the ready. James withdrew three tin cups from the back of the wagon. "You're a little nervous, boys. Expecting trouble?"

"Just pour and don't ask questions. We're hired to do a job and we're not taking any chances."

After the heat of the day the night felt cool, but with the effect of the whiskey, it didn't take long for the two men to warm themselves up for the long night ahead. In fact, they must have thought it was going to get real cold, because they made sure they would be real warm. So warm and relaxed that they were soon fast asleep, and James moved the supplies down into the Camp of Jolly Creek while the rouges slept on.

To say the people of Jolly Creek were happy to see him would be the understatement of the century. It had been James' plan to unload the supplies and foodstuff at a distance, then get back up the road and by the two sleeping sentries before anyone was the wiser. Unfortunately such was not to be.

The people of Jolly Creek were a simple lot. Like shepherds throughout time they wanted little else than to be left alone to tend their flocks of sheep, moving from one area of good pasture to the next, seldom asking of anyone for anything but the bare essentials. But as simple folk tend to be, when given such a gift as James had brought them, they would not let him leave without showing their gratitude, not realizing that it may mean the death of him.

This is not to infer that they were so slow as to deliberately expose James to those that were sick. The sick were kept together in a tent away from the others, the less ill nursing the ones unable to help themselves.

Besides, the pox had run its course and those that had survived were regaining strength with each passing day. They would, however, carry the pox marks on their faces for the rest of their lives as a reminder of how close death had come to their door.

They insisted that he break bread with them at their evening meal, a meal they would not have had if not for James. James, of course, refused but they would hear nothing of it. Their pride was at stake, and pride can kill a man just as well as a bullet. To not eat would mean to take back with him what they were in such desperate need of--the food and medicine. Still James' intuitive nature told him he must get out while the getting was good. Those rascals wouldn't stay drunk forever.

James thought the best thing was to go along with the settlers' desires and hope there would still be time to get out before he was discovered. The way the two ruffians had guzzled the booze, he figured they were out for the count. Just how long the count was, no one could tell.

James had seen men drink themselves into oblivion, just to come to an hour later and go at it all over again. James wasn't too worried about the rat. He was all talk and probably out of action the rest of the evening. The big guy might be a different story. The way he was putting them down, it was plain to see he had had his fill of rotgut in the past and could probably handle it fairly well. The supper was lousy but done in the spirit of gratefulness. James thanked them for their hospitality then headed out with the wagon at a fast trot. It would be easy to keep to the road in the moonlight, but he would have to go cautiously by the guards for fear of waking them, if they weren't already awake and waiting.

Coming up on their position he could see nothing moving in the darkness. Better be careful, he thought to himself. Reaching under the seat his hand found the long-blade knife he had concealed there earlier. He didn't want any trouble from the rat and his friend, but if it came to that he would give a good accounting of himself.

In the darkness he made out the two forms of the sleeping men. He took a deep breath and held it, the creaking of the wagon sounding like a cannon shot to his ears. Neither moved as he rolled by. He was just letting the airflow out of his lungs when out of the darkness a lone figure emerged and blocked his path. The man had stopped to have a drink with his friends before heading for his ranch a few miles away, and had rode up just in time to see James start up the road with wagon.

In the moonlight James could see the glint of the rifle in the man's hands. "If you don't want to have to explain to my friends over there what you been up to, then you better turn your rig around and go back down to them sheepherders. It's either that or I can bury you right here! What's it gonna be?"

James didn't answer. Backing the wagon off the road he was soon on his way back down to the friendly folks at Jolly Creek Camp. James knew he couldn't stay at Jolly Creek, but with three men watching the only road out, there didn't seem to be much choice in the matter. He could stay and take his chances or he might be able to ride out some time in the night. He would have to leave the wagon behind, it wasn't much good anyway having come with the price of the horse.

For now he'd find a place to sleep and once rested would think the matter through. He also thought it would be better to keep out of sight of the gunmen. After making fools out of them, they may want a little revenge and he would make too good a target from where they were perched on the high ground.

The cask of whiskey was a small one, but would still take several men a couple of days of hard drinking to finish off. James knew that a drunk with a rifle was a bad situation at best. Give that same man a reason to get mean and you had a nightmare on your hands, for sooner or later he would erupt and start shooting.

James drove the wagon around to the side of the cook tent so that it stood between the wagon and the sentries on the road above. Rolling his jacket up for a pillow, he was soon fast asleep dreaming of home and his family hundreds of miles away. It was a nervous sleep, and he woke every few hours thinking he heard hoofbeats coming down the road from above.

The morning came with the usual activity of people doing chores and washing up for breakfast. Jolly Creek, like other sheep and cow camps, had its own cook responsible for all the meals for the little community of shepherds.

With the pox on them, the guards on the road above, and all their sheep gone, the people had nothing to look forward to each day. If not for James, they would have been in dire need of food, too. The creek provided all the water they needed so that water was not of concern to them.

James rolled over in the wagon to let the sun warm him a little. At this time of year the days were warm, sometimes becoming uncomfortably hot. But the nights cooled quickly and without blankets of his own, the night air had chilled James clean to the bone.

"Hi, when did you come back?" The little girl with curly, blond hair stood waiting for James to answer. James stretched his arms and let out a yawn.

"Never did get to leave last night. That bacon I smell cookin'?" James' stomach growled. "I guess I could use some at that. It's been a long, cold night."

The little girl skipped away toward the cook tent while James got up and stretched, then walked over to the creek to wash up. He was just reaching into the cool, clear water when an explosion of water and spray sent him scrambling for cover.

He dove into the first tent that offered shelter from view of the men on the hill above. Pulling the flap back ever so carefully he peered out. There on the road was the moose and the rat with a rifle in his hand. They were both laughing.

Give me a cannon and I'd teach those buggers a lesson or two, thought James. A cough brought him back to reality. There setting at two large tables were the inhabitants of Jolly Creek. A man at the head of one of the tables came forward and welcomed James.

"Mr. Templer, we're all very sorry for the trouble we have brought upon you. Last night we all thought you had somehow gotten permission to bring us the supplies. Now we realize you were risking your life for us and we are very grateful to you."

"You didn't ask for my help, it was my own doing so don't feel bad. If there is a way out, I'll find it. I may need your help at that time, but for now that food smells awful good."

The man led James over to the table where a plate had been placed for him, while a woman came and filled his cup with coffee.

"Around here we all help ourselves with the food from the stove. Please feel free to take whatever you want. Thanks to you there's plenty."

James thanked her, then took his plate over to the stove. There were biscuits in a large frying pan with a bowl of gravy alongside. On a large griddle several pounds of bacon were frying. The cook asked James how he wanted his eggs.

"Just scramble a couple up for me," James replied. While the eggs were cooking, James started up a conversation with the cook by asking him how long he had been with the sheep men.

"About eight months now," was his answer. "I learned to cook in the east and decided to take a wagon train out to California where we ran into some trouble with the Indians. Lost everything I owned except the griddle here and a few pots and pans. Got me a job cookin' for an outfit trailin' cows down to Mexico, but quit after a few weeks. Got tired of the cowhands shootin' everything up.

"When we crossed trails with the shepherds, I joined up. They were on their way to California and I thought it would be worth it to come along with them. For the most part they're a peaceful lot. Everything was goin' fine till the pox hit us. Now they've lost everything, too.

James studied the eggs on the griddle. "How'd all the dents get in your griddle here?" he asked. The cook flipped some bacon over, then wrinkled his nose.

"Like I said before, the cowhands would come in all wild eyed and start shootin' everything up. One night this crazy saddle tramp came in, said I tried to poison him. Pulled his six-gun out and started blastin' everything up. Then he got a mean look in his eye and said he was going to kill me.

"There wasn't any place to run so as he stepped in close to shoot me, I jerked this griddle up and held it between us. He fanned his gun at me, being too drunk to realize what he was doing. Put four shots into the griddle and the fifth in the water barrel. It happened so fast that the force of the bullets pushed me right back against the chuck wagon and held me there.

"When his gun was empty, I hit him over the head with the griddle. Killed him deader than a doornail. I guess you could say I owe my life to this here flat iron. Anyway, the dents don't seem to hurt the cookin' so I guess I'll use it a while longer." James thanked the man for the food, then took his place at the table. The grub hit the spot.

"What do you plan to do?" the man beside James asked after a while.

James thought for a minute then shook his head, "I don't know, but I'll think of something before too long." He got up and took another peek at the men above. "Do you suppose they were trying to kill me this morning when they shot at me by the creek?" The man came over to where James was looking out of the tent.

"You see that small one up there? He's the one you have to watch out for. He was the one that did the shooting this morning. I don't think he was trying to hit you, just scare the heck out of you instead."

"Has he shot anybody so far?" James wanted to know.

"One for sure, and probably the other one as well. Course, none of us saw that one, but we had a ringside seat for the last one. That was the time he killed Abel's son. You met Abel at breakfast this morning." James nodded his head in the affirmative.

"Would you mind tellin' me what happened?" The man looked over his shoulder to where Abel sat with a few of the other men.

"Come outside so Able can't hear, he's been through enough already." He opened the tent flap for James to go through. Before James moved he took another look at the men on the hill. They were paying little attention to the camp below, and James guessed they were probably finishing the rest of the whiskey off.

"Lead the way." They came to a bench along the side of one of the tents and sat down.

"About three weeks ago Charles, that's Abel's son, was a headstrong young kid of about seventeen. We'd been here about a week, and it was obvious the gunmen weren't going to let us out. This kind of played on Charles' mind. To make matters worse, when Charles would walk partway up the road they would stop him and yell threats and sometimes taunt him. Of course, they always had a rifle covering him.

"So one day Charles, without warning, saddled one of the few horses we had left and charged up the road. The smaller man waited until poor Charles was but a dozen feet away, then raised his rifle and shot Charles through the heart killing the poor lad instantly. They allowed some of the men to come up and get his body. His is the second grave over there."

The man pointed toward the cemetery and a grave with a small handmade cross on it. James felt the sadness that the whole camp must have felt at the loss of Charles.

"You say that he waited for the boy to get a few dozen feet away before he shot him?"

"That's right, it looked like he was going to make it. It looked like he was going to be allowed to leave, then at the last minute the man, that scum up there, shot poor Charles one shot through the heart. He didn't have a chance.

"It was a great shock to the camp, and Abel I don't think will ever get over the loss of his son. In fact, we had to restrain Abel for a couple of days after Charles' death to keep him from trying the same thing. It would have been useless. Those men up there are cold-blooded killers and they have no intentions of letting anybody escape from here."

James agreed with that last statement. The murderers on the hill would let no one live to tell what they had already done.

"Earlier you had mentioned that they had killed another man that tried to get out of here. Is that true?"

"I'm afraid it is. After the rancher came and saw our situation here in camp, they warned us not to try to leave this valley. At first they seemed kind and like they wanted to help. The next day we heard shooting on the plateau above.

"We had left the sheep there with a Judas to keep them from straying. Abel and some other men headed up the road to see what was happening when they were stopped by the gunmen. They did, however, get a look at what the ranchers had done to our sheep. Killed every last one of them. They were all most of us had. If we do somehow get out of here, where will we go?"

James looked at the man, feeling the hopelessness the man must feel. "I don't know, I just don't know. But one thing's for sure, the cattlemen owe you people for all your sheep they destroyed, and if my hunch is right, there'll be a big reward for those two up there. You and your people could start over with more sheep, maybe a ranch of your own."

The man started crying. "How would we, a peaceful people, get out of here, let alone collect a reward on those two? We would have to kill them and we have no guns, no weapons of any kind! Even if we did have, we are no match for those murderers. We are shepherds, not gunmen."

James drew in a long breath. "I will kill them for you!" he said.

The man took a hard look at James, "No! They will kill you first."

James ignored what the man had said. "Now finish telling me about the second man they killed."

It was as James had suspected. The man had been shot through the heart at close range. Some men have written signatures. Artists use their own styles, a signature so to speak. If James was right, the rat had a signature of his own--a shot through the heart at close range. If this was in fact true, then James had all the edge he would need.

"I appreciate your telling me what you did, now I've got some things to work out." James left the man at the bench and headed for the cook tent. A short time later he emerged, looked at his watch, then up the hill. Next he went to his wagon and got a short piece of rope and his Army overcoat. Carrying these, he disappeared back into the cook tent. When anybody tried to enter, they were stopped at the door by the cook.

When James came out of the cook tent, he was wearing the long blue overcoat around which was fashioned his gun belt. It looked kind of odd, this tall stranger dressed more for the cold of the winter than the warm days of spring.

"Now, you remember what I told you. If everything works out, then get everybody out of here as fast as you can. Once you're all out, get over to the nearest marshal's office and make a report about what happened here. Be sure to check on any rewards for those men up there. I'm sure there'll be one!"

"What if you fail, then what?"

James smiled at the cook. “Then you’re on your own. Just give me a good burial.” The two men shook hands and James mounted up, checking his handgun one last time.

“Here take this,” the cook said as he handed James a long-bladed knife in a boot sheath. “You might need it.” James slid the knife down into the inside of his left boot.

“Thanks and good luck,” he said before turning his mount toward the road and galloped away.

The rat was the first to see him coming up the hill. “Well, well, what do we have here?” The moose got up and came over, handing the rat his rifle.

“They sure don’t learn, do they? What’s he dressed like that for?”

“Maybe he thinks if he gets all dressed up in his pretty uniform we’ll allow him to order us around and let him out of here. I think I’ll just put a nice neat little hole right where that pretty brass button is right over his heart. I’ll let him get just a little closer.”

James saw the rat bring his rifle up and knew he was about to get fired on. Right through the heart rat, don’t get sloppy now, shoot me right through the heart.

James kicked the horse into a fast run as his hand went to his gun.

A puff of smoke came from the Rat's rifle, and a split second later the bullet tore its way through James' coat where an instant before the big brass button had been. James was lifted up and back helpless to do anything. In slow motion he saw his horse run out from under him and on past the rat and moose. He was falling--down, down into a gray darkness. The last thing he saw was the moose coming down the road to where he lay. Then everything went black.

Slowly the air filled his lungs and his senses returned. He was being rolled onto his right side. He opened his eyes to find the moose on top of him going through his pockets. Their eyes met and the moose went for James' throat. It was useless for James to try for the gun at his side.

The moose had rolled James over it and the gun now lay pinned under him out of reach. James remembered the knife the cook had given him just in case, and his left hand found it where he had placed it a short time before in his left boot. With one powerful thrust he shoved the blade up under the big man's rib cage.

James felt the warm blood flow out and over his hand and arm. Still he pushed, turning the blade as he did so. The big man's hold loosened on James' neck and he was able to breathe again. The man's eyes closed and James knew he as dead.

"What's takin' you so long?" the rat called. "You find somethin' I should know about? Maybe tryin' to keep it for yourself."

James peeked from under the dead man's arm and saw the rat advancing toward him, the rifle still in his hands. Now James had a real problem. In order to get his gun he would have to roll off his right side, allowing the rat to see that the moose was dead.

James wouldn't have a chance but he must get to his gun. The moose wasn't wearing one, and the rat held the rifle at the ready. The only thing he could do was let the rat get as close as possible without giving himself away. If James was lucky he could roll the moose off of him and grab for his gun.

The weight of the man on top of him was becoming unbearable. James had a throbbing pain in his chest. He almost screamed at the rat to hurry it up, but held back. Now the rat was just a few short steps away. He held the rifle directly at James. The only thing between them was the hulk of the dead man. The rat levered another round into his rifle and pulled it up to his shoulder. Did he know the moose was dead?

"Get off him and bring me what you found or I'll drill you one right in the back!" the rat roared. James knew it was now or never.

With all the strength he had left, he rolled to his left pushing the dead man to the side while at the same time going for his gun with his right hand. The rat was quick and James' gun had not cleared leather before a bullet slammed into the same spot where James had been hit before. Right over the heart!

Blackness was coming fast, and through the fog in his mind James heard himself scream, "No! You bastard!" Another shot filtered through his brain, then nothing. James was dead.

"Hey, wake up!" James looked out through a mist. Is this what it's like to be dead? He felt himself being violently shaken.

"Open your eyes, you're alive! You did it!" Someone patted his face.

"No, I'm dead, let me be."

Again a pat on the face. Reluctantly he opened his eyes. The cook was bent down beside him, a kind smile on his face.

"James, you did it, you got them both!"

"I did?" James could not believe he was still alive, let alone that he got both men. "I heard the shot, I couldn't have gotten them. He shot me twice on the ground."

"No, the last shot was yours, you got him right in the heart."

"The heart? I shot him in the heart?" James let out a laugh. "That's funny." Then everything went black again.

He awoke back in the cook tent. "What happened?"

The cook brought over a cup of coffee, "Here, take this, it'll make you feel better."

James took the offered cup and drank. "Now I remember. I was riding up the road and got shot, right?"

"Right, he got you through the heart or so he thought. Hit you twice, the first one knocked you off your horse. The second one was while you were on the ground. I wonder what went through his mind just before you shot him."

"He probably thought I was the hardest man to kill he had ever met. I'm just glad he didn't decide to shoot me in the head."

"Amen to that!" The cook lifted the griddle off the floor where it had fallen after being cut loose from under James' heavy blue coat.

"From the look of this, and the blood on your shirt front, you were mighty lucky anyway."

There in the griddle was a small hole in the spot that had been over James' heart. "That last bullet went through. It was lodged just under your skin. You bled some but it's stopped now. If he got another shot at you, it would have been curtains for you." James stared at the hole for a long while.

"Did it ruin your griddle?"

"I don't think so, I'll just have to cook around the hole is all."

"It's a good thing for that."

"Why?"

"I'm hungry."

Chapter XI

John Templer was tired and hot. The dust of the desert made him thirst for the cool rivers of his home. The sun overhead dried everything in sight and made illusions of great lakes in the distance, but the great need in his heart made him go on when he might have given up miles before. He knew Jolly Creek was somewhere to the north of where he now sat. But where? The only directions he had received were to follow the infrequent signs placed along the trails.

He had found a sign laying along the trail. It was placed where the trail branched out into several paths each going in a different direction. John had chosen the one that went toward the north. Now miles further down this path, it had yet to reveal the location of Jolly Creek. In fact, there were no more signs along the way and no creek far as the eye could see, only the vultures circling in the distance.

From experience John knew that the great birds of death only circled when there was food at hand. Could this be an omen that he would be too late getting to Jolly Creek? And what of James? Was James safe or was he part of the food the vultures expected to soon eat? John rode on, his gut tied in knots. A constant prayer in his mind, Lord, let my boy be alive!

The ground was harder to follow now, the trail being just a trace of itself from a few miles back. John had to ride with one eye on the ground ahead and one on the birds in the sky a few miles away. When the trail turned away from the direction of the birds, John rode straight ahead, treading his way between sagebrush and mesquite, keeping a careful watch for the occasional rattlesnake that might lay in wait under a rock along his way.

The birds were almost overhead when John noticed the land dropping off to reveal a small valley below. He reined up so as to look around. If this was the place he was seeking, then there should be some gunmen close by, and he had no wish to be seen before he could spot them.

Dismounting he walked closer to the edge and scanned the rim around the valley below. No one was visible so he let his gaze fall to the valley floor. There below was a creek of crystal clear water cascading down the hill and through the valley floor to exit by a small notch at the far end of the valley.

The whole valley couldn't be more than half a mile across from where John was standing. Crossing the creek was a rutted wagon road that climbed up and out somewhere to the south. There was nothing else to be seen below him except the unmistakable shape of the cemetery.

John felt a sick feeling creep over him as he analyzed the scene below. He was sure this was Jolly Creek, but it lay barren with not a living soul to be seen anywhere, only the cemetery to show that life had existed here at all. It was almost more than John could take. If James had been kept prisoner here, like he had heard the rest of the camp was, he would have found a way to free him--gunslingers or not.

John knew how to deal with those kind but now to find nothing, no one. Where had they gone? John looked at the graveyard again. Were they all here? Was James here, too? He knew he must find out; he must know what had happened to his son.

Half running, half falling, he was soon down at the bottom of the hill. The road was off to the side from where he was by a few hundred feet, so John waded the creek, the cold water feeling good against his legs. He did not stop to refresh himself but went straight to the cemetery and a spot where two fresh mounds of dirt lay waiting in the sun.

The little graveyard held about seventeen graves as far as John could tell, but only two of them showed by the darkness of the dirt to have been dug within the last week or so. Scattered around the ground were so many discarded items of tinware and clothing. Amongst these was a long blue overcoat with big brass buttons. A name tag sewn inside the collar caught John's attention. He bent down and picked the coat off the ground. Where there should have been a brass button there were now a couple of nice neat holes caked with what John knew to be blood.

He turned the coat around in his hands until the label inside the collar caught his attention. It read: James Templer, Captain U.S. Army. John grasped the coat to his breast and cried. There at his feet in one of these graves was his son James.

There was nothing more for John to do but to get Ruth and go home. Before leaving he said a prayer for his son and the other unfortunate souls in the little graveyard at Jolly Creek.

Looking about the area it was easy to tell where the tents had been pitched by the way the ground had been trampled smooth by many feet. Still clutching his son's overcoat, John started across the creek. I have come so far only to find nothing left of my boy, he thought. I wish I could trade places with him. John Templer started the long climb up the hill to his horse.

James let his horse lope along at its own pace. It felt so good to be alive and on his way home at last. Seeing the clouds in the far-off hills he wished he had brought his overcoat with him instead of forgetting it back at Jolly Creek.

But no matter, he still had money left over and he was sure to pass through a town in the next few days. He could buy what he needed then. For now he would enjoy the sunshine and sweet air. He had plenty of water in his canteen, it being at least half full, and a fast horse under him.

And he was alive! He hadn't felt so good, so free, in years and he was going to enjoy every bit of it. Even the fact that he was on horseback couldn't ruin the day for him. He would have rather been on the seat of his wagon, but he had to leave it for the shepherds to move their camp with.

Ahead, he could see some dust on the horizon, probably from a stage or maybe a band of riders. Could be Indians but James didn't think so. It would be highly unlikely that they would stray this far south this time of the year, but he would keep a wary eye open for any trouble ahead just the same.

He kicked the horse into a gallop and was just settling back for the ride when the horse abruptly fell out from under him. James was pitched high and hard, and when he hit the ground it was with a crash that knocked the wind out of him. He lay there trying to get his wind back and was finally able to get up.

The sight he saw made him sick. His horse lay on its side, the femur in his left leg protruding through. James wanted to cry. The realization that he was lost miles from nowhere hadn't dawned on him yet. He was only aware of the fact that here was a poor animal that moments before had been gracefully moving along without a care in the world, now reduced to a scared, miserable beast that would have to be put to sleep, the victim of a prairie dog hole.

Someday, somewhere he thought, they will be able to fix a horse's broken leg, but for now there was only one thing for James to do. Drawing his gun from its holster, James moved behind the horse's head. Talking in gentle, soothing tones to the animal, he aimed at a point just behind the ears at the middle of the horse's head and fired. The animal jerked once, then lay still. Tears rolled down James' face as he unfastened the saddle and bridle from the dead animal.

In the sky overhead the vultures were already gathering for the feast that would soon be theirs. James watched them in disgust. "If I had a shovel, I would bury you to keep you from them," he told the dead horse at his feet, "but I don't, so they will have their way with you. I'm sorry."

James looked around him. If he had been in a rowboat far out at sea it could not have seemed worse. He was at least twenty miles from the nearest ranch house. It was hot with no water except what he carried in his canteen. Once the sun went down there was sure to be snakes in abundance.

He kicked himself for even thinking about trying to go cross-country, especially country he was unfamiliar with at best. Maybe if he had been more used to the lay of the land he would have had enough sense to stick to the roads.

James knew there was no time to waste. He couldn't carry much and he felt it would be useless trying to find his way back to this spot if he did get out alive. He would have to take only the bare necessities and leave the rest of his gear behind.

Now what way to go? He had been headed northeast figuring to cut some miles off his way home. It was a different story now. A man alone out here couldn't last long without a horse and water, and James had only a limited supply of one of these. He began to worry.

Dust blown up by the wind began to settle around him. His blue shirt and pants took on the look of a uniform of the Confederacy covered as it was with the gray dust of the desert. Wouldn't do much good to wipe it off, so taking his kerchief and placing it over his nose and mouth James walked on mile after mile, hoping to cut a road or settlement.

His water was low, not more than a few mouthfuls left when he spotted the dust raising in the distance. Could it be from Indians out on a scouting party, James wondered. He watched as the cloud thickened and moved closer.

If it was Indians they would have to be moving at a steady gallop and James knew that Indians seldom moved cross-country at more than a walk, saving their horses in case they needed them for an attack or to save the Indians from being attacked. Whatever it was, it was moving too fast to be a wagon train, so that left only one thing--a stagecoach.

James felt hope for the first time in hours, but he knew that it was still a long way off to whatever road the stage was on. Also, this might be the only stage through this way for several days.

He guessed the distance between him and the stage to be somewhere between ten and twelve miles. Judging by the dust trail it might come within one or two miles of the spot where James now was. Could he make it in time? James didn't know but he was going to give it one hell of a try.

Uncorking his canteen he quickly swallowed the rest of the water, then set off at a fast trot, throwing the canteen to the side. James was in good shape except for the wound he had suffered a few months earlier, and it was pretty much healed, just leaving him a little stiff in the shoulder.

On he ran, stopping every so often to check on the dust cloud moving ever closer. The last time he stopped he could see that the dust trail was close, too close, and would pass him by a mile or more. James almost gave up in frustration. He sat down in the dirt and put his head in his hands letting the futility of it all rise up and completely consume him.

Then something inside made him take one last look at the dust cloud that he knew would be passing far in front of him. It wasn't where he expected it to be. Instead, it was now coming toward him and off to his left. James could not believe his eyes. In an instant he was on his feet and running. This time he ran for all he was worth. He reached the road only fifty feet in front of the stage.

Bursting out onto the road, he was almost run over by the lead team of horses. The dust being thrown up by their hooves blinded him to all else and he had to throw himself back to keep from being run over by the coach. Then the realization came that the stage didn't even slow down.

James wiped the dust from his eye and watched as the stage disappeared in the distance. This time it was too much for him and he let the tears flow from deep within as he sat down in the middle of the road to die. James was fully aware that without a horse or water, he could not survive another day out here alone.

The rumble of the ground brought him to attention. There coming toward him from the direction it had just gone was the stagecoach. Getting to his feet he waved and yelled as hard as he could but it was hardly necessary, for the stage was already coming to a stop in front of him.

"Whoa!" the driver yelled as he brought the team to a standstill beside James. "You scared the daylights out of my horses when you came running out in front of them like you did. You mighta' been killed pulling a darn fool stunt like that. What you doing way out here anyway?"

"Lost my horse cutting cross-country, drank all my water. Guess it was a fool stunt at that."

"Well, get on board, can't keep the regular fares waiting while I pick up every fool on the road. Better climb up here with me, at least till the dust blows off you." James thanked the man, then started to climb up when he was stopped by a voice from within the coach.

"Did I hear you say you haven't had any water for a while?"

"Yes, sir, and I'm mighty thirsty at that." The door of the coach opened and a big muscular man dropped to the ground and turned to face James. He had a water jug in his hand. The two faced each other, then the big man spoke. "You sure look like someone I know, though he would be a mite younger."

James didn't speak. He tried but nothing would come out. Finally the words came. "Pa? Is that really you?" John Templer's face took on a look of shock.

"James, is that you, James? We thought you were dead. Oh, my Lord, it is you!" John threw his arms around his son. Now both men had tears in their eyes. “Ruth, come quick! It’s James, it’s James! He’s alive!”

Ruth stepped out of the coach and watched as the two men approached her. Then in an outburst of emotion she ran to her son, tears streaming down her cheeks.

The driver looked down on all the commotion in wonderment. Finally grasping the situation he set the brake and climbed down from the coach where he soon produced a bottle of fine bourbon.

“Listen, folks. I don’t mean to be buttin’ in, but this here calls from some sort of toast. So if I wouldn’t be offendin’ anyone, I’d like to toast your good fortune.” The Templers all looked at the man, then broke out in laughter.

“We’d be honored, sir,” John said. A big grin spread across the skinner’s face as he opened the bottle of bourbon.

“Been savin’ this for just such an occasion.” He passed the bottle to Ruth first. “Ma’am, I don’t have any glasses so maybe you better drink first.”

This brought another round of laughter, then Ruth took the bottle. “I don’t usually take to men drinking licker but this is one time I don't mind if I do." With that she tilted the bottle up and took a long pull.

John and James looked on in amazement. They had never seen Ruth drink anything stronger than punch at one of the socials back home. Ruth let the booze slide down easy then handed the bottle to the driver who took one big gulp and passed it on.

There would be so much to talk about and John and Ruth were anxious to hear everything that had happened to James.

Chapter XII

A knock on the door brought Sam to his feet in a hurry. Before opening the door he checked to make sure the gun he held in his hand was loaded. Josh took a position by the window where he could look out without being seen by whoever it was at the door.

"It's the telegraph kid," Josh told his older brother. Sam put the gun down and opened the door.

"Hi there, young feller. What can I do for you today?" Sam smiled at the little boy on the front porch.

"Got another telegram for you, sir." He handed Sam the envelope with the telegram in it, then turned to leave.

"Hey! Wait a minute, young man. You had a long ride out here and you deserve something for your trouble. Here, take this!" Sam handed the boy a big, bright nickel. The boy turned it over in his hand and smiled back at Sam.

"Thank you, sir," he said, then climbed back on his pony and rode off still looking at the nickel Sam had given him.

“What’s it say?” Josh asked, as he crossed the room to where Sam stood.

Sam opened the envelope, almost afraid of what it might read. “It says: “Found James alive. Be home Saturday 27. Send our love. Signed John Templer.”

“Alive! It says James is alive!” The two men let out a wild yell of celebration, then both bowed their heads and thanked the Lord for being so merciful and good.

“Come on. Let’s saddle up and go tell Henry the good news. Maybe Doc will let him come home before the folks get here. The 27th is almost two weeks away.”

Josh agreed with Sam and within a few minutes they were riding out toward Doc’s house. On the way Josh mentioned to Sam that they were running low on a few things and he thought it might be a good idea to stop by town on the way back to restock.

“Sounds all right to me,” Sam agreed.

Before long they were telling their little brother the good news. Doc had to warn them several times not to get Henry excited or they would have to leave.

Henry needed to rest and the Doc was going to make darn sure he did.

Henry himself was regaining his strength and felt well enough to go home, but the Doc said not for another week, then he would see. The fact that Henry had lost an arm didn't seem to bother him all that much. In fact while Josh and Sam were there, he would often make jokes about it.

At first the doctor thought it was a cover up, that Henry was subconsciously denying the fact that he lost his arm. But as time went on the doctor was able to see that Henry was really dealing with his injury in a mature and conscious way. The jokes were an attempt to make everyone else feel better. Yes, Henry had come to grips with the loss of his arm, and because of this the doctor was sure the boy would have a quick and full recovery.

The closer to town Sam and Josh rode, the more nervous Josh became. He had good reason to be nervous with all that had transpired in the last few weeks. One thing had been learned in recent days: the man who called himself the judge was really kin to the Horsteads and not a judge at all.

Whether the man had left the country or not was still to be answered. Vern had sent word for the boys to be on the lookout just in case he might still be around planning something else.

"I wish I would have brought a gun along just in case we run into trouble," Josh said.

"I thought you might be thinkin' that way so I brought one for you. It's in your saddlebag. Vern said to give it to you. It's his old .32 caliber revolver. Said you're a man now and wanted you to have it. A present from your godfather." Josh reached back and retrieved the nickel plated six-shooter from behind him.

"There's a holster and belt in the other bag. Go ahead and strap it on if you want." Josh smiled at the sight of the little gun in his hand.

"You sure it's all right?" he asked his older brother.

"Sure. In fact Vern recommended we both be wearing sidearms when we come to town. Said there's a lot of talk that some of the Horsteads might still make trouble for us, thought we better be prepared."

"That's all right with me. Ya think Pa will let me wear it when he gets home?"

"Just have to wait and see. After he hears what's happened and sees Henry, he might decide to wear one himself."

The closer they rode toward town the more Sam noticed that Josh seemed to be getting more nervous. "You all right?" he asked Josh.

"Sure, why?" Josh asked.

"You seem to be nervous. Something on your mind?"

"Nothing important, I was just thinking about the man that was impersonating the judge. I was wondering whether Vern has found him yet. Do you think he's still around here?"

"I was wondering that myself."

The men rode on in silence, watching over their shoulders and riding well out from any place where someone could be hiding in ambush. Reaching town they rode down the back street and pulled up behind the general store.

"We better go in the back way and see what's happening. If any of those Horsteads are about, Jones will know. One of his customers would be sure to say somethin' to him."

The portly man was busy behind the counter when Josh and Sam came in. "Well, I'll be, how you boys been? Sorry about your brother, Henry. Saw Doc this mornin', said he'll be up and around any day now."

"Mr. Jones, do you know if any of the Horsteads are around? We're not looking for any more trouble, so if they're here we'll just get on back to our place."

"No need to do that, the only Horstead in town is Mary Jane. Boy, she looks plumper than a watermelon." Josh winced at that last remark.

"As a matter of fact, she said something about needing to see you, Josh. Course, folks here in town all heard what happened to Henry and they don't listen to any Horstead. Matter of fact, they never did!"

"Where's she now?" Josh asked. The rotund man behind the counter pointed a plump finger toward the boarding house.

"Got herself a room over there."

"She there now?"

"Don't rightly know, you could always go over there and ask Mabel, she'd know if the girl was in or not."

"No thanks! Don't have anything to see her about anyhow." The fat man looked Josh over, then went back to sweeping the floor.

"Leave your list and I'll have your supplies in an hour for you. You ride horseback or bring the wagon?"

"Horseback."

"I'll pack your supplies in a couple of sacks so you can throw them over your saddles."

"Thanks. We'll see you in about an hour." Sam motioned Josh out the door.

"What do you suppose Mary Jane wants to see you for?"

Josh got a lump in his throat. "I think I know, but it's not important."

"If you say so. Let's go over and get some grub."

"Not at Mabel's boarding house!" Josh stated.

"Boy, something's got you spooked. No, not at the boarding house. Flarty's serves up a good meal and the price is right, too. That all right with you?"

"Sure."

"Then Flarty's it is." An hour later the men were again at the general store after eating a meal of hot roast beef served up with hot biscuits, mashed potatoes and all the coffee they could drink.

"Got all your supplies tied up for you, Sam. Say, Vern was in here a few minutes ago looking for Josh. I told him I thought you might have gone to the boarding house for a meal."

"We were over at Flarty's."

"Anyway, Vern said it was important he talk with Josh before you go, said he'd be in his office."

"Did he say what he wanted Josh for?"

"Nope, not a thing, but I suspect it has something to do with the Horstead girl."

Sam turned to his brother, "Come on, Josh. If Vern wants a word with you, we better go over to his office and see what it's about."

Josh followed Sam out the door and across the street to Vern's office. Inside Vern was making coffee, he looked up as the two men entered.

"Hi, Sam, Josh. I was hoping you two would drop in before you left town. How's Henry doin'?"

"Pretty good, considering all he's been through in the last couple of weeks. Jones said you wanted to talk to Josh, so here he is."

"Sam, maybe you had better give me a chance to talk to Josh alone."

"I'll go get a drink," Sam offered. "Be back in a few minutes, that give you enough time?" Vern got to his feet and moved across the room to where Sam was.

"That'll be just fine. Thanks, Sam."

After Sam left, Vern had Josh sit down across from his desk. After a long pause Vern started, "Josh, I don't know how to say this, after all that you and your family's been through. I guess the only good thing that's happened in the past few weeks is that James is alive."

"How'd you know that?"

"The telegraph operator told me. Anyway, I guess the best way to say what's on my mind is to say it straight out. Mary Jane Horstead said you are the father of her baby! Josh, I'm your godfather and I wanted to ask you before it got around town. Are you the father of the baby?"

Josh didn't know what to say. So much had been going on in his life. Now he was being asked if he was the father of a baby whose mother had the worst reputation in the county.

He looked down at the floor unable to speak. A sick feeling spread into his stomach. In a very small voice he replied, "I may be. I don't know for sure."

Vern came around the desk and laid his hand on Josh's shoulder. "Josh, she said you raped her. She wants me to arrest you."

"Are you going to?"

"On her word, no way! But what I am going to do is find out just what she or her family is up to. One more question, then you and Sam better get back home and let me work this out."

"What's the question?" Vern walked around to face Josh, then cleared his throat. The last thing in the world he wanted to do was to ask Josh the question he was about to ask.

"Josh, did you rape her?" Josh looked up at his friend.

"I don't know. What's it mean to rape someone?"

Vern looked at the innocent looking young man sitting before him. In his heart he knew Josh would never do anything like that.

"Josh, I know you well enough to know you're not guilty of rape, so you better get on home. Sorry I had to ask. Now I've got someone to see."

"We'll head for home as soon as we pick up our supplies."

As soon as Josh was out of the office, Vern went looking for Mary Jane. He found her at the old three-story boarding house known as Mabel's.

"Sheriff, what are you doing here?" she said as she stepped into the hall pulling the door closed behind her, but not before Vern saw the boots by the bed in her room.

"Sorry, Mary Jane, if you got company I can come back some other time."

"I don't have no company, sheriff. What makes you think I would? You trying to blame someone else for what that Josh Templer did to me?"

"No, ma'am, I'm not trying to blame anyone at this point, just trying to get the facts."

"Why, sheriff, I already gave you the facts. Josh Templer raped me then killed my father. I'll see him hanged for one or the other."

"You listen to me, young lady!" Vern hated to call her a lady. "You aren't going to see anyone hanged. You know as well as I that your pa tried to kill Sam Templer and it wasn't Josh's fault that your pa was killed. As for whose baby you're carrying, that remains to be seen!"

"The only thing to be seen is Josh behind bars!" Mary Jane screamed.

"Speaking of bars, where's that cousin of yours, the one who played judge and got Henry shot, not to mention several other men killed?"

"How would I know?" she said defiantly.

Vern pointed his finger in Mary Jane's face as a warning. "You know more than you're sayin' and when I get to the bottom of this, you're going to be in a lot of trouble."

Mary Jane started to say something then thought better of it. Instead she opened her door and quickly stepped inside, trying to slam it in Vern's face. Vern was too fast for her and caught the door before it closed completely.

"One more thing, Miss Horstead. If I find out that you were behind that cousin of yours trying to have Josh and his brothers killed, your baby may be an orphan soon after it's born. The law in this state says that anyone that tries to have someone killed is just as guilty as the person that does the actual killing."

A look of defiance spread across Mary Jane's face. "None of the Templers were killed, so what are you talking about anyway, sheriff?"

"Lawyer Phillips was telling me that if someone causes another to be killed, then they're guilty of that person's death and can be tried as such!"

"You must be gettin' old, Mr. Kelso. You just said that and I told you nobody was killed, so what's your point?"

"Point is, several men were killed trying to attack us at the water hole. Before one of them died he said that the judge, meaning your cousin, hired him and the others to kill Josh and his brothers. If they hadn't been hired for the job they would not be layin' up at boot hill now. You see, Mary Jane, somebody has to pay for sending them out to get killed."

Mary Jane's face went pale and there was a slight tremble to her voice as she spoke. "I didn't have anything to do with any of that! I just want the man that raped me, and that's Josh Templer."

Vern let go his hold on the door allowing it to close, but not before he noticed the boots were gone. He had to move fast if he was going to catch whoever owned those boots. He knew whoever it was would have to come out some time and he figured it would be right after they were sure he was gone.

The boarding house had two stairwells. One went down to the front of the house where the family room was and was used most of the time by the guests coming and going. The second set of stairs went down the rear of the house to the back door. The door at the back of the house was usually kept locked to keep unwanted guests out.

Vern figured whoever it was in Mary Jane's room would take those stairs to keep from being seen. What Vern would have to do is leave by the front stairs, then hurry around to the back in time to catch whoever was up there with her.

Vern walked over to the stairs and started down, then stopped. Behind him he heard a door snap closed. Vern guessed it was Mary Jane watching him leave so her guest could also go but by the back stairs where they would not be seen.

Vern hit the front door at a run. The boarding house was one of four houses built in a row. Between the boarding house and the two houses on each side was a high fence with no gate. Vern cursed himself for forgetting the fences. Now he would have to run all the way around a second house to see whoever came down the back stairs.

Rounding the corner of the second house, Vern burst into the alley behind. No one was in sight. Vern walked over to the back door, it was open. He was too late. One thing though, Vern knew he would remember those boots. And he was sure whoever was wearing them had something to do with this whole mess.

It was no use trying to find the person wearing the boots. They could be anywhere by now. Vern turned around and walked back to his office disgusted with himself for being out of shape. If he had been a little quicker he might have the answer he was looking for.

For now there was nothing left to do but wait and watch, hoping a clue might turn up. Then he noticed the envelope on his desk. Opening it he read the telegram inside. It read: "Will arrive tomorrow. Mary Jane Horstead charges rape. Have defendant Josh Templer ready to answer charges. Signed Justin A. Page, Circuit Judge, Bexler County."

Vern couldn't believe what he was reading. Josh Templer would have to stand trial for rape! Ever since Mary Jane made her accusation of rape, Vern had an uneasy feeling about her motives.

Mary Jane came from one of the scroungiest families anyone dared lay eyes on, although she wasn't so bad. In fact, she was like a breath of spring to someone standing knee deep in a manure pile. She was for the most part clean and well kept. That was on the outside. On the inside she was just as contemptible as the rest of her family, maybe even more so.

If there was one thing Vern was sure of, it was the fact that the last thing someone would have to do to

Mary Jane Horstead was rape her. It was said that Mary Jane was willin' most any time of any day or night. It was also said that she wasn't choosy either.

So why was she wanting to cause Josh all this trouble? Was it because Josh had killed her pa? Vern doubted it. She and her pa had been going at each other as long as anyone could remember. Even if she had been raped it still didn't mean that this baby was the result of it, like she was trying to say it was. There had been just too many lovers for her to be able to say for sure.

Vern remembered just a couple of months before when he was out making his rounds, that he had scared Mary Jane and one of the local boys. Mary Jane had told him at the time that she had a bug down her blouse and the boy was just trying to get it out. Vern might have fallen for it except it was the front of her blouse he had his hands down. Now that he thought about it, there were a lot of stories floating around about Mary Jane and the boys.

What about the boots he saw in her room? They certainly weren't Josh's, so who's were they? Why had she sent for Judge Page? Judge Page, why that old goat wouldn't know the truth if it hit him in the mouth, or so he was told by a peddler just this morning.

The boots kept coming to mind as Vern sat there wondering what to do next. Find the owner of them and he'd find the father of the baby, of that Vern was sure.

He got up and went to the window. Across the street he saw Josh and Sam's horses tied to the hitching rail. Vern took one last look at the telegram, then grabbed his hat and went over to tell Josh the bad news.

Sam was the first to see him come in. From the look on Vern's face he could tell something was wrong.

"What's up, Vern?" Sam asked.

"Just got a telegram from a Judge Page. Seems that Mary Jane Horstead sent a wire off to him charging Josh with rape." Vern turned to face Josh. "Josh, it's out of my hands now. The judge will be here tomorrow and wants you handy. I hate to ask you to stay, but I've got to. The judge ordered me to keep you here."

"Did he order you to arrest Josh?" Sam wanted to know.

"Not in so many words, the wire just said to have Josh ready. But if the judge thinks I didn't arrest

Josh, then he'll not listen to me when I speak in his defense. He can sleep on the deputy's cot in the corner.

"Josh, you better come along with me now. You can bet that Mary Jane's watching our every move, and if she thinks something's amiss, she'll report to the judge first thing when he gets here."

Josh looked to his brother for advice. Sam nodded in agreement with Vern. "I'll spend the night in town, after we get this out of the way we'll ride home together. That right, Vern?"

"That's right, Sam. Josh will be all right, I'm sure of it." Vern hoped he sounded more confident than he really was.

Chapter XIII

The rumble of the stage was like a soothing song to the three members of the Templer family. The stress of the last few weeks had taken its toll on James and his parents, and now traveling along behind a strong team with the countryside sliding by outside, it was easy to sleep. With the curtains drawn closed, only a little dust found its way into the coach to bother the occupants inside.

They had been traveling through open plains of tall grass with scrub trees dotting the landscape. Now the dusty road took a turn east and began a long, gentle climb to the mountains a few hundred miles further on. John pulled the curtain back and looked out at the world they were passing through. The sun was setting behind them, causing the shadows to grow long, making eerie visions ahead on the road. But still the stage bore on, covering mile after mile of jarring rock-strewn rutted road that first twisted one way then another, never settling into one direction for more than a few hundred yards at a time.

The hot heat of day turned cool, then cold as the sun slid behind the mountains to the west taking with it the last rays of light and warmth. Inside the coach, the Templers were pulling the blankets from under the seats and using them as shield from the cold.

The driver in the box above had already taken precautions against the cold by placing a heavy leather cover over his legs to break the wind. With his hat pulled down low over his upturned collar, he cursed the darkness then gave the horses their head, letting them pick their way over the trail they had traveled so many times before.

The team sensing the change in the reins took charge as though knowing the responsibility thrust upon them to deliver the coach unerringly through the night. With flared nostrils they ran on, pulling their charge toward its destination and their own reward of rest and grain.

A few miles ahead a man crouched behind a boulder beside the road. He had not counted on the stage being so late. Now that it was getting dark he reassessed his plans. Originally he hoped to stop the stage when it was slowed to a crawl for a rough area in the road. He had checked for miles without finding the spot he wanted, a spot that would have allowed him to hail the driver and force him to stop and hand down the cash box, while at the same time providing enough cover to keep hidden from view of the driver and passengers.

Such was not to be. If there was such a place it was miles away, and the outlaw could not wait another day. He was getting more desperate by the minute. He needed money now--money to eat on and to get out of the country with.

He knew that by now he was being hunted for murder, so it was now or never. His new plan was to jump out in the road with rifle in hand, stop the stage, shoot the driver, get the cash box and rob the passengers of whatever they had that he could use, then kill them, too. By the time the stage was reported missing, he would be miles away.

He would head for the coast and board a ship out of the country. In a few years when all was forgotten he could return and start life anew. Who knows, if there was enough cash on the stage, he could invest it in the Orient and maybe come back a wealthy man. Of course, he would have to change his name. The thought tickled him--come back a wealthy and respected man. He knew that wealth could always demand respect and he would demand plenty.

In the distance he heard the stage coming. Soon he could vaguely see the stage coach's silhouette coming toward him against the lighter background of the horizon. It would be touchy, he thought. Make my move too soon and the driver would be warned in time to defend himself. He would have to step into the road at the last moment to keep surprise on his side.

The stage was growing nearer. The man poised himself, rifle in hand, black hat pulled low over his face. Almost, just a little closer, almost there.

Now! He jumped into the road, but the stage didn't stop. The horses bore on, not seeing the man dressed all in black. The first horse knocked the man down while the second and third horses in line ran over him. It was not until the wheels of the coach ran over the inert form that the driver knew that anything was even wrong.

"Hold up you muleheads!" he yelled while pulling hard on the reins. The horses ground to a halt.

"What's up, driver?" John called up.

"Don't know yet, think we hit something in the road back there, might have been a man."

John got out and jumped to the ground. "I'll walk back with you if you don't mind."

"Don't mind at all, might need your help."

"You really think it's a man?" John asked, as he felt his way over the uneven ground.

"Can't say for sure, but I think it was a man. Course, may be a mountain lion. If we find that's what it is and it's still alive, I'll let you grab its tail and hold it back."

"Hold it back from what?"

"From catching me, I'll be running the other way. You can let it go after I'm whipping the team down the trail."

"What about me?"

"Mister, all you have to do is ride the cat up to where we'll be waiting. I figure by that time you'll have it pretty well tamed."

The man let out a belly laugh that almost shook the ground. John wasn't laughing. He had almost tripped over the body of a man dressed in black. The mule skinner came up beside him and spit, then wiped his mouth with the sleeve of his jacket. "Looks like we ran over a judge doesn't it?"

Chapter XIV

It had been a long night and Josh was still tired when the smell of bacon woke him. He rolled over to better see where the smell was coming from and rubbed the soreness out of his neck at the same time.

"Smells mighty good," Josh said to Vern who was busy by the old wood stove in the corner.

"Thought you might be a little hungry after all the tossing and turning you did last night. Want milk or coffee with your breakfast?" Vern asked, as Josh wiped the sleep from his eyes.

"Milk, if it's handy. If it isn't, coffee will do." Josh got up and crossed the room to where the wash basin was.

"Am I in a lot of trouble? What I mean is, could I be put in jail if the judge believes Mary Jane?" Vern gave the eggs a turn then wiped his hands on a rag beside the stove.

"Josh, I didn't want to tell you until you had a chance to eat and get cleaned up, but I guess this is as good a time as any." Vern motioned Josh over to the table where two plates were set.

"This judge that's coming to hear the charges against you isn't someone to fool around with. The way I hear it, he lost his wife a year ago. She was murdered by some drunken cowhands that came up from Texas."

"What does that have to do with me?"

"His wife was raped first by all four of them, then they carved her up. The judge found her as they had left her. They say he's never been the same since. And now that Mary Jane has charged you with rape, he may seek revenge for his wife by being doubly hard on you."

"I don't understand why he would want revenge from me. I never did anything to him or his wife, or Mary Jane for that matter." Vern slid some eggs and bacon from the pan to Josh's plate.

"Start eating, while I try to explain it to you. You see, when a man loses something that he loves, as the judge did his wife, he sometimes hates anything that reminds him of what took his loved one away. His wife was raped, and now you are going to have to prove you didn't rape Mary Jane. If we can't prove that to his satisfaction, he may take out some of his hate on you. Do you get the picture?"

"I see what you mean, but I didn't rape her."

"We know that, and so does Mary Jane, but she's going to try to convince the judge and jury if it comes to that, that you did rape her and that she's carrying your baby. Why, I don't know, but if it's the last thing I do, I'll find out!" Vern sat down and hurried through his breakfast.

"I've got some things to do before the stage gets here. You best stay here and keep out of sight. I'll send Sam over to keep you company. If your folks come in today, I'll send them right over. But first, I'll fill them in on what's going on."

"Where's Sam now?" Vern shrugged his shoulders. "I hope he's not trying to talk to Mary Jane. It could only make things worse."

Sam was finishing breakfast when Vern came in the front door of Flarty's Hotel. Vern pulled a chair up to the table, then ordered a cup of coffee.

"I'm glad you're here," Vern began, "I was afraid you might try to talk to Mary Jane. The judge wouldn't like that, and it could make things worse for Josh."

"I wanted to but thought better of it for those very reasons. By the way, I talked to a drummer this morning who says he knows this Judge Page. Said that he hangs people for rape. Is that so?" Vern took a swallow of coffee.

"I don't know the man personally, but from his reputation I'd say that's pretty much right."

Sam's face grew cold, his voice came out hard. "I'll not let anyone hang my little brother! 'Specially for something he didn't do."

Vern sat there in silence knowing full well that Sam meant what he said. Sam was the first to break the silence. "What time's the stage due in?" Vern took his watch from his pocket and looked at it.

"It's due about eleven-thirty. That gives us about forty-five minutes to wait." Both men sat in silence, lost in their own thoughts.

The stagecoach was five minutes early. Vern heard it come past as he and Sam sat at Flarty's. Sam had started to get up at the sound of the coach going past, but Vern reached out a hand and stopped him saying, "I may need you later to find some answers for me. It might be better if the judge doesn't get a look at you yet."

Sam was hesitant to stay but finally agreed on the condition that Vern keep him informed on anything important. Vern agreed, then left for the stage depot, secretly hoping the judge would not be on the stage.

If he could stay away just one more day, Vern was sure he would be able to find the owner of the boots he had seen in Mary Jane's room the day before. Once he found the man he was looking for, Vern felt he could get the answers he needed to free Josh from the charges. Such was not to be.

By the time Vern arrived at the station old Pete Rodriguez was already unloading the rear boot of the stage. No passengers were in sight, so Vern assumed them to be inside waiting for their baggage.

Pete greeted Vern loudly, "Hi, sheriff. What you in such a hurry for?" Vern just waved back as he went inside to find the judge. It was dark inside and it took a moment for Vern's eyes to adjust to the light.

"Are you looking for me?" came a strong voice from the darkness. As Vern's eyes adjusted, he found before him a medium-sized man with silver white hair. He was clean shaven with eyes that cut right through a man. After many years as sheriff, Vern had developed a sixth sense about people. And what that sense was telling him now was that the man before him was no pushover. He was his own man.

"I'm Sheriff Kelso," Vern offered, as he held his hand out to the judge. The judge immediately took it but he did not smile or change his expression at all. Vern was surprised at the power of this man. In the many years he had held the Office of Sheriff, Vern got to know many judges.

Most were on their way to one higher office or another. Some were good, others weren't much better than the people they presided over. Most were soft, fat little men who ate too much, and when not on the bench, drank too much. Some even drank when they were on the bench, which always made Vern mad, but there was little he could do about it.

This man was different. He was neither fat nor soft and he emitted a confidence that Vern hadn't felt from any of the judges he had known in the past. The man's easy smile made you want to trust him right from the start.

"I'm Judge Page, you can call me Justin if you like, except in the courtroom, of course. I have a few bags, so as soon as they are unloaded we can get on with the hearing."

"You mean right now?" Vern was more than a little surprised at the judge wanting to convene court so soon. After all, he had just gotten into town.

"Of course, right now! No use spending any more tax dollars than we have to. The stage won't be leaving for another two hours. If we can get the matter resolved before then, I can be on my way.

"I'm paid to be a judge, and I've never seen anyone get much work done while waiting in some out of the way hotel. If you can get the complaining party over to court, then all we need is the prisoner."

Vern didn't like the term "prisoner" being used in this case. "Look, Judge, there's some things you ought to know. First of all, the prisoner as you put it, is only a boy. I've known him all his life. In fact, I'm his godfather and I know he couldn't force himself on anyone."

The judge folded his arms in front of him then coughed to clear his throat. "Sheriff Kelso, am I to understand that you believe this boy to be innocent?"

"Yes, sir, that's about it."

"And you further believe that this boy, as you put it, couldn't force himself on anyone?"

"That's right!"

"You are sure of that, Sheriff Kelso?"

"Judge, he's only a boy and a good boy at that." Justin reached his right hand into his breast pocket and brought out a small leather bound notebook.

"Then why, Sheriff Kelso, did this good boy, as you put it, on or about the tenth of this very month kill several men in a shootout?"

Vern was flabbergasted that the judge had knowledge of the ambush already.

"Judge, I myself was in that same shootout. Josh's little brother lost an arm at the same time. Josh did what had to be done. If not for him I would not be alive today. The others started it by trying to ambush us."

"Others? Who were the others, sheriff?"

"Doesn't your book tell you their names?" Vern was getting irritated, both at the judge and at himself for making such a mistake about this man. He thought about what the peddler had to say about the judge being off his rocker. In view of the conversation he was having, Vern had to agree.

"Sheriff, if it did, would I be asking you who they were?" Vern blushed with anger.

"They were some men hired by a man who pretended to be a judge like yourself." Vern looked the white-haired man in the eye.

"And now that I think of it, how do I know that you are who you say you are?"

"Quite simply, by asking for my credentials." The man fumbled in his breast pocket again, this time bringing out a thick, black wallet. He opened it and took some official looking papers out. He handed these to Vern.

"As you can see, I am who I say I am. You can read, can't you, sheriff?" Vern handed the papers back to the now smiling judge, then turned and walked away without answering the man's insult, but the judge would not be put off so easily.

"Sheriff, I'm not done talking to you yet!"

"Yes, you are!" came Vern's reply. The judge just chuckled as Vern sulked away.

"That man's got either a temper or he truly believes the boy's not guilty," commented the judge to himself.

Vern was mad--mad at himself, the judge, and most of all at Mary Jane for getting Josh in so much trouble. What was she up to? After her father's death she hadn't seemed too upset. It was common knowledge she and her pa were always at each other's throats. Vern wouldn't have been the least bit surprised if there had been some incest between them.

There had always been the question if he really was her pa. Most of the townspeople believed otherwise. Vern doubted that she was seeking revenge. After all, Josh had done her a favor by killing old man Horstead. Everybody knew that. Vern just hoped that Mary Jane also felt the same way, but what could it be that she wanted enough to destroy a young boy's life?

Vern pulled his watch from his pocket. It was now five to twelve, just a little over an hour and a half before the stage pulled out. Not much time to prove a boy innocent of the charges that had been brought against him. Vern knew he must try, for Josh's life was held in the balance.

Vern wondered if he would be able to get anything out of Mary Jane. With the judge setting up court in just a few minutes, it didn't give him much time to even try. But he knew he must, Josh's life depended on it.

Mary Jane was in the outhouse in back of Mabel's, Vern was so informed by an indignant Mabel. "Vernon Kelso," she had said, "can't a body even go take a nature break without you wanting them for something?" Vern quickly apologized while keeping an eye out for Mary Jane when she emerged from the little building in the back of Mabel's boarding house.

"Another thing, sheriff. It may not be a good idea to get that poor girl all excited. She looks to me as though she's going to have her baby any time now."

"Great, just great!" cringed Vern. "That's all I need, a boy on trial for rape and the accuser is going to have a baby right before the judge's eyes. Damn! Well, tell her that the judge is here and wants to get on with the hearing as soon as she can get over to the courthouse."

"Tell her yourself, she's coming out right now." Sure enough, Mary Jane was coming toward them in what could only be described as a waddle. To Vern it was as though she had grown twice the size in just a few hours.

"Mary Jane, I have to talk with you," he called. Mary Jane stopped and looked in his direction. Putting her hands on both sides of her stomach, she seemed to lift the burdensome load of the baby and came to where Vern and Mabel were standing.

"What you want, sheriff?" Vern felt uncomfortable addressing the pregnant girl, especially when that girl was Mary Jane Horstead.

"I came to tell you that the judge wants you over at the courthouse as soon as you can get there."

"Is that so? He does, does he?"

"That's what he told me to tell you. Of course, you being in the shape you're in, I'm sure he would understand if you wanted to put the hearing off for awhile." Vern was hoping for more time but he wasn't going to get it.

"You and Josh would like that wouldn't you, sheriff? Just tell the judge I'll be right over!" Vern tried to look concerned for Mary Jane's health.

"But Mabel was telling me you might have the baby any time now. Don't you think it would be better to wait until next week, after the baby's born?"

"I'll be right over!" With that Mary Jane waddled into the back door of Mabel's.

"You should have insisted!" exclaimed Mabel.

"You heard her, she wants to get it started right now. Believe me, if there was any way I could have stopped her, I would have."

Mabel looked very concerned, "Sheriff, that girl just might have that baby any time now and she doesn't look too good. Now, I'm no doctor, but I've seen a few babies born in my day and I'm tellin' you, she's a sick child, that one is!"

By now Vern was losing patience with Mabel. "Just what in high heaven do you want me to do about it, Mabel?"

"I'm sorry, sheriff. I know you're under a great deal of pressure right now with Josh Templer in trouble like he is. It's just that I'm worried about the baby and I kind of forgot how serious things are."

"I know you are, Mabel, but the fact is she just isn't thinking of the baby right now. She's thinking about convicting Josh of a crime I'm sure he never committed. Beats me why."

"Would you like me to send the Doc over?"

"That might not be such a bad idea. Thanks, Mabel."

Josh was already at the courthouse when Mary Jane arrived. She looked no better than when Vern had seen her fifteen minutes earlier. As she entered she glanced around the room, her gaze halting on Josh as he sat facing the judge's bench. She was still holding the excess weight of the baby with her hands. Her complexion was flushed and she was breathing hard.

It was a few seconds before Josh saw her. As his eyes met hers, she quickly broke off contact, but not before Vern caught a strange look of remorse on her face. He was sure that he had seen it, and felt if he only had more time he could break down her story and save Josh.

Mary Jane waddled down to a seat in the front row of the courtroom. Soon others followed. Vern could make out several members of the Horstead clan. The rest were just curious townspeople.

Before long, Judge Justin Page came in and the people stood up until he was seated. The air seemed hot and stuffy and Vern motioned for his deputy to open a window. Vern guessed there were about twenty-five people in the courtroom when the judge brought the court to order.

All fell silent except for the heavy breathing of Mary Jane. The judge seemed not to notice. Vern wondered how anyone could keep from hearing Mary Jane, for she now was letting out little gasping sounds.

"This court is now in session," came the cry from the deputy who was also acting as bailiff, "The Honorable Justin Page presiding."

"Is the defendant present?" asked the judge.

"I am," said Josh in a low voice.

"Do you have counsel, young man?"

"I am Mr. Templer's lawyer, your honor," answered Jay Phillips.

"Your name, sir?"

"Jay Phillips, Attorney at Law"

"Does the plaintiff have counsel?" asked the judge again.

"She does, your honor," said a slim man in his late twenties.

"Then who might you be?" queried the judge.

"Sir?"

"What's your name? You do have a name, don't you?"

"Yes, sir, it's Perceval W. White the Third." Several snickers went up in the courtroom.

"Well then, Mr. White the Third, and you, too, Mr. Phillips, since this is only a hearing you won't be needed today."

"But judge!" Lawyer White protested.

"That will be all, Mr. White. You may leave the courtroom at once or I may find you in contempt of court. Do you understand?"

"Yes, sir!"

"Fine. Now get out! You, too, Mr. Phillips!" As soon as the two flabbergasted men left the room the judge began again. "Now that that's out of the way we can begin to get to the bottom of this. First off, Mr. Templer, please come forward."

Josh shot a glance over at Vern who motioned Josh to go up to the judge. It did not escape the judge's eye.

"Mr. Templer, I know you are not used to being in a courtroom. So I will explain how things work. When the judge asks something of you, he means for you to obey without getting permission from someone else, not even the sheriff. Have I made myself clear, Mr. Templer?"

Josh felt the tears well up in his eyes. Not even when he had faced the gunmen did he feel so scared. He took a deep breath and held back the tears. "Yes, sir."

"Fine. We can get on with the hearing then. Now, Mr. Templer, did you ever rape this girl?" The judge pointed across the courtroom to where Mary Jane sat.

"No, sir, I did not rape her." The judge smiled down at Josh.

"Fine. Now will Miss Horstead come before me. You, boy, can sit down."

After several attempts Mary Jane was able to gain her feet. But after a few steps it was obvious that she would not make it any further.

"Sheriff!" the judge ordered, "You better help the girl, I think she's in some difficulty."

Vern jumped to his feet just in time to catch Mary Jane from falling. The judge asked Mary Jane if she would rather wait until after the baby was born to finish the hearing.

"No!" she screamed. "I want it over with now! My baby needs to have a name, legal and proper, when it's born."

So that was it. Mary Jane was accusing Josh of rape so her baby would have his last name. A name from one of the most respected families in these parts. Everything fell into place for Vern now. Mary Jane had despised her family from the start. She had hated everything they stood for. Now, when she was about to have who knows who's baby, she was making a last ditch try to give it some respectability, even if it took destroying Josh in the process.

"Young lady, do you mean to tell me you want the name of the man you're accusing of rape for your baby?"

"Yes!" cried Mary Jane as she slumped to the floor grasping her stomach. "I want his name."

The judge moved from behind his desk to a spot beside Mary Jane. The doctor had already come in and was now working to make Mary Jane more comfortable.

"Get some sheets, she's going to have the baby right now!" ordered the doctor.

"Am I going to die?" whimpered Mary Jane. The doctor bent over her and was about to answer when the hand of the judge on his shoulder stopped him.

"You're in pretty sad shape, Mary Jane. You better make your peace with your Maker now while there's still time."

The doctor looked up at the judge as to ask what he was doing. The judge tightened his grip on the doctor's shoulder almost causing him to wince from the pain.

Mary Jane was in tears, making little gasping sounds through each contraction. "Oh, God, what can I do?" she wept. The judge moved in closer to her so that he was now in front of the doctor.

"You are going to a far greater Judge than I. Better answer me, than He." Mary Jane was now gasping for breath. Her forehead was covered with sweat, then all at once she became calm.

"What do you want to know?" she asked.

"Did Josh Templer rape you?"

Mary Jane started crying. "I may have raped him, but he did not rape me," came the surprising answer.

"Then who did rape you?"

"No one!" she began crying.

"Then who is the baby's father?"

Mary Jane rose up on one elbow. Wiping the tears from her eyes she looked about the people standing around her. "I only wanted my baby to have a chance in this world."

"Who, Mary Jane? Who is the father of your baby?" the judge demanded.

Mary Jane took a deep breath, then lifting her voice she said, "That no account Jack Redding!"

Jack who had been standing a short distance from Vern made a run for the door. Vern bolted after him. Vern was quicker than Jack this time.

Sure enough, it was Jack Redding who was wearing the boots that Vern had seen beneath Mary Jane's bed at Mabel's. Vern dragged him up to where Mary Jane was lying on the floor.

The judge spoke again. "Why did you blame Josh Templer?"

"A name, I wanted a good name for my baby." She started to bawl again.

"I didn't want the baby, I'm no good. I thought if the Templers thought it was their grandchild they would take it in. I didn't know that Josh might die, I only thought of the baby. And now I'm gonna die."

"No, you're not," the doctor cut in. "You're going to be a mother."

"I don't want the baby!" she cried, not yet fully comprehending what the doctor had just told her. All eyes turned to Jack Redding.

"Don't look at me, I don't want it either!" he said in mock defiance.

The judge was now on his feet. He took charge again.

"I am inclined to agree with these two children. They have not the mentality nor resources to care for a baby." He addressed Mary Jane. "Young lady, are you sure in what you say? You do not want this baby you are about to have?"

Mary Jane looked him right in the eye. "Look at me. I'm a tramp and I'll always be a tramp. It would be better for the baby if I died!"

The judge suddenly appeared to become kind and understanding, the harshness of voice of a moment before changed to one of soothing, almost tranquilizing softness. He bent down close to Mary Jane. "Mary Jane, would you be willing to adopt your baby out to a nice home?"

"Oh, yes, judge," she pleaded. He looked up at Jack Redding.

"Is that all right with you?" he asked. Jack shook his head yes.

"You must answer me clearly, Mr. Redding. Is that your wish also?"

"Yes, it is, sir."

The judge got to his feet and went back to his desk. "Doctor, do you want some help moving her to the boarding house?"

"Yes," he replied.

The judge appointed some men to help the doctor. "Now the court will again come to order. Inasmuch as the parents of the about to be born infant have agreed to adoption, I now order that by the power invested in me, the newborn will be taken away to be placed in adoption as soon as it is born and a good home can be found for it."

The judge sat back and looked around the room. "Are the parents of Jack Redding here in this courtroom?" No one came forward. The judge waited, then saw Vern's raised hand. The judge smiled. This unnerved Vern but he kept his hand up. "Yes, sheriff, what is it?" Vern came forward until he was just a few feet from the judge.

"Sir, Jack only has one parent and he's locked up in jail for being drunk and disorderly. It's a constant problem for as long as I can remember."

"Oh, I see. Then I suppose the grandfather wouldn't want the baby either. In that case, after the baby is born, if any of the townspeople want to adopt it and can show me that they would be good parents, I will allow it. Until then, I will be spending the taxpayers' money on a room at the hotel until this matter is resolved."

"We'll take the baby, your honor!" came a booming voice from the back of the room. There, framed by the double doors, stood a big man, his clothes covered in dust from a long journey. His features as sharp as though chiseled from granite. His wife stood beside him, a pretty women, her hand in his, her firm mouth set off by loving eyes.

"Sir, we don't even know what the child will be yet--boy or girl.

"I said, 'we'll take the baby!' We don't care what it will be. It will need a loving home, and that's what we will give it. Now, you just make out whatever paperwork we'll need."

The judge involuntarily started to write when he stopped himself.

"Wait a minute! I don't even know who you are! How do I know you would give it a loving home?"

The big man moved forward with a grace not often seen in men as big as he. "Judge, my word's as good as any piece of paper you can write. My name's John Templer, and Josh is my son."

The judge held out his hand to John. John hesitantly took it.

"The baby is yours, Mr. Templer." Justin looked over at Josh who by now was with his mother. "I suppose you will want to have a few words with me about how I treated your boy. Things were not as they might have seemed, Mr Templer, but if you want to say your piece I'll listen," John grinned.

"I sure do! I and the boy's mother want to thank you for helping our son clear himself."

Justin Page relaxed a little. "Then you know about me, and what I was doing?"

"Sure do. It was your friend, the so-called drummer, that lent us his wagon and team so we could get here sooner."

"Your friend is the drummer? The one that told everyone you were nuts?" Vern asked, astonished at the very idea.

"That's the one," the judge smiled.

"Why would you want him to do that?" Vern demanded. Justin took Vern's arm and led him away from the Templers so they could get reunited.

"As you know, I'm not the regular judge in these parts. You see the governor wanted me to come down and get things back to normal after the war. There's so much work to do, and so little time, that I needed an edge. You following me all right?"

"Yes, I think so."

"By sending my friend as the drummer in ahead to spread rumors, it takes people off guard and I'm able to get to the bottom of things pretty fast. You'd be surprised how many bribes I'm offered to hang some innocent man."

"Well, I'll be. But couldn't it get dangerous for you? Lots of gunslingers around that might use you for a target."

"That's been tried, too. I guess that's why Mama, I mean my wife, insisted I wear this." Justin pulled back his long black coat to reveal a Colt .44 in a tied down holster.

"She must have been a fine lady," Vern said.

"What do you mean 'must have been'? She still is," the Judge said.

"You mean to tell me she's still alive! She wasn't raped and murdered?"

"Of course not! That was just part of the false rumor to throw people off guard. And it worked too. Fooled you, didn't it?" Vern looked at the judge.

"It sure did. I thought you were going to seek revenge on anyone you could."

Vern was flabbergasted by everything that had happened. "Justin, I got to hand it to you. You had me fooled, but aren't you afraid someone might call you out in the street for a shoot-out? There can't be a sheriff around all the time to protect you, and you must make a lot of people mad in your line of work."

Justin Page laughed. "You think I wear this for looks?" touching the gun on his hip. "I'll tell you a little secret, but you got to keep it to yourself."

"I can do that."

"I used to be a U.S. Marshal before growing older and settling down with a fine woman. She talked me into getting better educated and becoming a judge.

You may have heard of me back then. They used to call me, Justice."

"You're Justice, the lawman?!" Vern asked. "I never put it together!"

"Not many people do. I've aged some and put on a little extra weight since then. But I still try to protect the innocent as well as convict the guilty. Same job, just don't have to get out and roll around in the mud anymore." The judge let out a laugh. "Anyone tell you this town has a lot of crows?"

Vern was puzzled at the sudden question. "Why do you say that?"

The judge didn't answer, but instead looked skyward. "There's one now!" In a flash, too fast to follow with the human eye, Justin's right hand darted upward in a blur of motion, followed by a resounding boom. In the split second it took Vern to make out the shape of the crow speeding overhead, the judge had drawn and fired. Vern saw the bird disintegrate before his eyes.

"Judge," Vern said with admiration, "You're the fastest I ever did see."

"That's what Mama says," he said with a wink. "Here's a dollar." He flipped the silver coin to Vern.

"What's this for?"

"Shooting my gun in town," the judge said. " I fined myself a dollar. Tell John Templer I'll send the paperwork to make the adoption legal tomorrow on the next stage. Speaking of the stage, I have one to catch!"

The End

Author's note: The baby was a girl!

CPSIA information can be obtained at www.ICGtesting.com
Printed in the USA
BVOW08s0045190614

356800BV00011B/164/P

9 781469 95